"You sa<del></del> *husband died," Mark began slowly. "But it's over."*

He wasn't asking. She hesitated. She could lie and say it wasn't, use that as an excuse for not seeing him again. But after the kisses they'd shared before, she knew that he knew she wasn't pining for another man. "It's over," she said, her voice a mere thread of sound.

All he said was, "Good," as he drew her close and bent his head to hers.

It felt so good, this coming together. She could feel the strength of his legs, the power of the arms that held her, the gentleness of his hand as it caressed her skin. Nothing had ever felt this good before, and she wanted it to go on and on.

She opened dreamy eyes and met the deep blue of his gaze. He kissed her with little darting movements before taking her lips in a powerful, searching assault that made her moan deep in her throat.

She had to close her eyes to keep the look of enchantment on his face from sending her out into orbit.

"No," he murmured. "Look at me. Don't hide your pleasure from me. . . ."

WHAT ARE *LOVESWEPT* ROMANCES?

They are stories of true romance and touching emotion. We believe those two very important ingredients are constants in our highly sensual and very believable stories in the *LOVESWEPT* line. Our goal is to give you, the reader, stories of consistently high quality that may sometimes make you laugh, sometimes make you cry, but are always fresh and creative and contain many delightful surprises within their pages.

Most romance fans read an enormous number of books. Those they truly love, they keep. Others may be traded with friends and soon forgotten. We hope that each *LOVESWEPT* romance will be a treasure—a "keeper." We will always try to publish

LOVE STORIES YOU'LL NEVER FORGET
BY AUTHORS YOU'LL ALWAYS REMEMBER

The Editors

LOVESWEPT® • 335

Judy Gill
Mermaid

BANTAM BOOKS
NEW YORK • TORONTO • LONDON • SYDNEY • AUCKLAND

MERMAID

A Bantam Book / June 1989

If you would be interested in receiving protective vinyl
covers for your Loveswept books, please write to this address
for information:

Loveswept
Bantam Books
P.O. Box 985
Hicksville, NY 11802

ISBN 0-553-22009-8

Published simultaneously in the United States and Canada

PRINTED IN THE UNITED STATES OF AMERICA

O   0 9 8 7 6 5 4 3 2 1

One

She was not having fun. Jillian felt as if she were about to suffocate as she panicked and grabbed for the oxygen regulator the diver, Robin, held in his mouth. Willingly he gave it to her, allowing her to take a couple of breaths. Then, holding one of her shoulders in a large hand, he took the mouthpiece back and breathed from it himself while he reached down and picked up the flashing lure that drifted near the bottom of the ocean. As rehearsed, she held onto his shoulders, and he let her have another breath or two. Then he retrieved the regulator and carefully fastened the sharp hook into the sparkling fish skin between her breasts—only he wasn't careful enough.

She jerked away as he scratched her skin with the hook, and glared at him as blood oozed from the small cut. Behind his mask, his expression was apologetic, and his cold fingers touched her even colder chest once again as he made sure no further damage could be done by the barbed hook. Then, after buddy-breathing once more, he gave the fishing line a sharp tug. Blurringly, Jillian saw the line rise on an angle in front of her. She felt it go hard and taut before she started to be drawn upward steadily.

Shaking his head, Robin gave her the regulator again, holding her down, making it hard for the fisherman on the surface. With her hand tight in his, he went so far as to swim in the opposite direction from where the line was pulling her before he nodded and allowed her to rise toward the surface for just a few moments.

She wasn't anywhere near the spangled, glittering surface, when again he led her off on a tangent. First one way, then the other, drawing her down or off to the left or the right, and all for the benefit of the cameras and the man on the other end of the line.

Her eyes accused him. Wasn't this enough? Damn, but the water was cold! she thought, wishing she could get the whole, ridiculous thing over with by giving one mighty thrust of her tail and ascending. But she and Robin had a job to do, and they had to do it right—at least by Robin's standards. He was stage-managing the whole thing, and as an avid sports fisherman, presumably he knew how a fish was supposed to act.

However, did he know how a mermaid was supposed to act? Jillian had to smile as she handed him the regulator once more. Heavens, even she, the only mermaid in town, didn't know how one would act if caught on a fishing line. In reality, she supposed, if mermaids did exist, they'd simply unhook themselves and swim away. For a moment she considered doing just that then remembered how well she was being paid for her stint down in the icy depths.

Soon, though not soon enough to suit her, Robin let her rise a bit more quickly toward the silver glimmer of the surface, and she realized it was almost over. Robin waited as she took several more replenishing breaths from the air hose attached to the tanks strapped to his back. Then he patted her bare shoulder and gave her a thumbs-up before diving away toward the bottom. He would, she knew, return to the surface, well out of camera range, and climb aboard the Zodiac—his part in the production finished.

Hers, however, had just begun, and when she finally reached the surface and the broken, choppy waves, she realized it was going to be a lot more difficult to maneuver with her tail than it ever had been in the depths of her tank. She was in trouble.

Waves caught under the tail driving her forward, smashing her face into oncoming swells. Coughing, sputtering, she stroked powerfully with her arms trying to force the tail to stay under control. But even though it was weighted to have negative buoyancy while underwater, it misbehaved badly above in rough water. There was only one thing to do.

Drawing in a deep breath, she aimed herself at the white blur that was the hull of the cruiser and dove down to where she could handle the cumbersome tail. There all she had to do was let the line pull her in the right direction and rise once in a while to gasp in a breath of air. If they needed film of her on the surface, surely they could patch in some clips of her taken in the tank.

Whatever it was, it was big. It was certainly the biggest thing Mark had ever hooked, and the weight of it on the far end of his line set his bare toes digging into minute crevices in the slippery shale rock where he stood. If it hadn't been for the fish's fighting, he would have thought that either his hook somehow had caught in the anchor line of the glistening white cruiser that lay a hundred feet offshore, or at least that his gear had tangled with that of the white-clad man who stood patiently on the stern, his back to Mark. But no, his gear wasn't hooked up with the other fisherman's; the man in white wasn't fighting anything. The man stood still, staring at the water as if he expected to catch something spectacular for the two cameramen who were poised, one on the bridge, one in a gently bobbing craft just off the stern.

Mark frowned, wondering who they were and why filming the man was so important. But his fish was fighting, and fighting so hard, it made him forget about the cameramen, the other fisherman, and the large white cruiser.

His arms and shoulders ached, and he felt veins standing out on his neck. This battle had better not be long, because it surely was a tough one, he thought, but when his line suddenly went slack, disappointment swept through him. He'd lost it. The granddaddy of all salmon, and it was gone.

While he slowly reeled in the slack line so that he could check his lure and hook, he glanced at the cruiser again. The cameras were still aimed out toward the entrance of the bay, and the man in white continued to wait patiently for a strike.

Thinking he had lost the fish, Mark was paying little attention to his line, when it snapped taut once more and ran off the reel, screaming as it went. He let it run for several minutes until the fish seemed to tire. Then, far out in the choppy blue waters of the bay, just off the bow of the white cruiser, a tail broke the surface—and what a tail! Broad, thick, blue-green and shot with silver, it slapped the water with a mighty splash before disappearing. The line slackened once more as if the fish, having showed itself, was now willing to come to Mark without a battle.

As he reeled it in slowly and easily, he kept his eyes on the spot in the water where the line disappeared. Suddenly the creature broached the water halfway between him and the white cruiser. He stared, gulped, feeling himself become lightheaded as an hysterical laugh caught in his throat.

No! He hadn't seen what he thought he'd seen. Or if he had, then he was crazier than ever. But oh, Lordy, there it was again—first the huge, shining tail curving up out of the water to land with a splash, and then . . . then the milk-white shoulders and arms, and sleek blond head with hair streaming down over a pair of sweetly rounded breasts . . . breasts covered with the same silvery scales as that massive tail.

He dropped the rod and reel, heedless of the line tangling around his feet, and simply stared, wondering if he was going insane. He glanced at the men on the cruiser. They hadn't seen it. Their attention was aimed at whatever fish the man in white had now hooked. He was straining at his rod, playing his fish expertly, and all at once Mark felt grateful that no one else was witnessing his rapid decline into insanity.

He didn't dare put a name to the creature that was swimming toward him. He could see her face, and it was lovely. Heart-shaped, it was as pale as her arms and shoulders, surrounded by the wet paleness of her long, straight hair. She was stroking strongly in his direction, her gaze clinging beseechingly to his face as she struggled to control the action of her tail in the choppy seas which caught it and swept it around, forcing her to dive under again and again. But her progress was steady.

His heart hammered high in his throat. He felt dizzy and wondered if he was about to pass out. No, of course not. He was not the kind of man who passed out. And he was not, repeat *not* seeing a mermaid. What he was seeing was some kind of hallucination brought on by worry, by overwork, by too much sun, by Lord only knew what. He was essentially a very practical man who did not believe in mermaids. So, of course, it was not a mermaid out there. Absolutely not!

But why did he feel sick to his stomach at the sight of the hook—his fishing hook—embedded in the scales between her breasts when she appeared on the surface to take a breath? He heard himself gag, and over the sound came the roar of a speedboat, which was full of teenagers and operating much too close to shore. The wake of the boat came sweeping in, caught that long, graceful tail, and tumbled the beautiful creature into the barnacle-encrusted rocks five feet below Mark's ledge.

He leaped down, landing in waist-deep water, and gathered her limp form in his arms. Lifting her clear of the surging swell, he saw a streak of diluted blood running from her temple to her cheek and neck, and more blood where the hook had entered. Feeling the coolness of her face against his shoulder, the roughness of her tail across his arm, the softness of the scale-clad breast as it pressed into his chest, the miracle of the impossible swirled through his suddenly very impractical mind.

He stared at her unconscious face for what seemed half a lifetime, a bubble of joyous disbelief welling up inside him. In his arms he held a mermaid! In his heart he held a moment's magic. In his soul he held a brand new world.

Then, becoming conscious of the icy feel of her skin, he knew he had to get her out of the water. Her lips were blue. He wondered if he should try mouth-to-mouth resuscitation but realized she was still breathing. Her head, though, was bleeding copiously. Her blood was sticky on his skin. The seawater streaming down his arm and side from her long hair was cold. The hook piercing her skin made him gag again.

He shuddered, cradling her more securely while scrambling up the bank. His knees were weak with shock, and the steepness and her unwieldy tail made the climb difficult. But when they were well above the reach of the water on the flattest part of the rocks, he stopped, bending to prop her scaly back on one of his thighs. Very carefully he took his knife and cut the leader, leaving only the hook embedded in her tender flesh, hoping she would remain unconscious until he could get her to a doctor and have the hook removed.

Doctor? Should he take her to a doctor or to a vet? he wondered with a false laugh. Or maybe to a marine biologist? Again, that mad little voice babbled in the back of his mind, and again he ignored it just as he ignored the loud shouts of the men in the cruiser who had finished making their film and were excited about the fish the man in white had caught.

He had a hell of a lot more than a mere fish to be excited about.

Lifting her, he struggled up the path toward the house, praying the cameras wouldn't by some chance pan his way. Once through the gate of the high, wrought iron fence, he closed it, relief washing over him at the sound of the lock clanging shut automatically. If anyone had seen what he'd caught, Mark knew no one would believe it. He didn't believe it himself, but in spite of that he didn't want to share his mermaid with the world, so he had to get her out of sight as quickly as he could.

He knew perfectly well that just as soon as she was well enough he was going to have to let her go and never tell a soul.

The thought brought him an unexpected jolt of pain. He didn't want to let her go. But in spite of everything that had happened, he was still a very practical man, and practical men did not make pets of mermaids—not even beautiful blond ones with sea-green eyes and tiny, golden freckles across their noses—he told himself as she opened her eyes and looked at him bewilderedly. He walked with her in his arms into the shallow end of his swimming pool.

As the warm water of the pool closed around her, Jillian let her eyes fall shut again. Where was she? Who was this man? Why was her head so fuzzy? She'd glimpsed eyes bluer than any sky she'd ever seen, the blue of real sapphires and a taut face wearing a worried expression. And there had been something else, but she couldn't think now, couldn't concentrate. She wanted to sleep where it was warm, where a hard, hot-skinned shoulder pillowed her head, and gentle, rough-skinned hands were moving over her face and neck and arms.

She wanted to . . . let the blackness . . . come back. . . .

Still supporting her, Mark dabbed at the blood on her temple and rinsed her face and neck clean. The cut wasn't as bad as he'd thought at first and would only require a Band-Aid. Sitting on the second step at the terraced shallow end of the pool, he cradled the mermaid in one arm and patted her lovely face, watching a hint of rosy color come into her cheeks. Her lips remained blue, and he wanted, with a shocking urgency, to kiss them to warmth. Wisps of blond hair were beginning to dry and curl in tiny, soft tendrils around her face.

Then, slowly she opened her eyes again and parted her lips as if to speak, but no sound issued forth. She frowned and lifted a hand to touch her wounded head.

"It's all right," Mark said in a tender tone he didn't recognize as his own, capturing her small, thin-boned hand and holding it. "You're going to be fine. You have a little cut on your head where you got bashed into a barnacle-covered rock. You'll have a small bump by the time an hour has passed, but it won't be too bad. You also have a hook in your . . . er . . . front that will have to come out."

She closed her eyes once more and rested on his chest as if that was where she belonged. Clearly she hadn't understood a word he'd said, but just as clearly she trusted him. It was a good feeling, he acknowledged, as he patted her cheeks again, saying, "Come on, beautiful. Wake up. Wake up, Mermaid."

He watched her tail give an experimental flicker of movement. Then, because he did not want to have to bring in a doctor, Mark quickly grasped the hook and gave it a turn, a twist, and a pull, stopping with it only halfway out when her eyes popped open and she gasped.

"Oh, Lord, I'm sorry," he said. "Sweetheart, I have to do it. I have to get that hook out of you. Please, stay very still. I'll be as gentle as I can."

Sweetheart? He had called her sweetheart? He, who had never called another woman that in his entire life, was calling a strange mermaid "sweetheart"—as if he meant it? Yes, he was. And it seemed right. He swallowed hard, steeled himself again, and once more reached for the hook.

To his surprise she pushed his hands gently away and then removed the hook herself with a quick flick of her fingers. Again he felt sick. He remembered all the fish he'd thought he'd hooked solidly but which had gotten away. How many of them had been—

My God! When had he started to believe in mermaids? Really and truly believe? Had he gone that far off the deep end? Was he so demented that he was really buying this whole thing? He stared at her and she stared back with faintly bewildered, sunlit, sea-green eyes. He never wanted to look away but knew if he didn't, something terrible was going to happen to him. If it hadn't already. He could feel his breath coming in short little puffs, his heart hammering high in his throat, his—

Hell! His eyes dropped to ripples in the water that hid where her legs should be. It was utterly pointless to get sexually aroused over a mermaid, for heaven's sake! Yet what was even more amazing, he realized with some shock, was that it had been one hell of a long time since he'd been aroused by anyone.

He also realized at the same moment, going weak with relief, that this was no mermaid in his pool but rather, a warm, vibrant woman who was looking up at him as if she knew exactly what he was thinking and feeling. And as if she didn't mind. As if maybe . . . she shared those feelings?

He was glad to know his sanity had returned, but if she didn't quit looking at him like that, he didn't hold out much hope for its lasting a whole lot longer.

Mark stared at her, for a moment feeling foolishly betrayed by the truth. He swallowed hard to rid himself of his childish disappointment, disappointment he knew he shouldn't be feeling because, of course, he'd known all along that there was no such thing as a mermaid.

"I have to leave you for a minute," he said. "You need a bandage on your head. I'll be right back. Then I think I should get you to a doctor in case you have a concussion." He loped away, and when he returned, she was looking a little brighter, her eyes more alert, her color better. Crouching beside her on the middle step of the pool, he gently wiped the blood from her head and dried the area with a towel.

"What's your name?" he asked after he'd afixed the bandage firmly to her temple. "And what in the world were you doing out there?"

Putting her hands on the top step, she pushed herself up one level and then hitched her body right out of the water onto the deck, leaving only her tail hanging into the pool. She smiled at Mark, showing small, even white teeth. He moved up to sit beside her.

"It's a long story," she said. "And my name is Jillian Lockstead."

He couldn't help it. He grinned. "I suppose your friends call you Jilly Fish?"

She laughed and flipped her tail, slopping water up over the edge of the pool. It washed across his lap, but since he was already wet, it didn't matter. Hell, with that laugh of hers ringing in his ears, he could have been bone-dry and dressed in a tuxedo and it wouldn't have mattered.

Her laughter was low and sultry and shockingly at odds with her delicate, fair looks. A laugh such as hers should have come from a dark-haired, red-sequined siren, Mark thought. But when he looked deep into her sea-green eyes, he realized that her voice and her laughter and her eyes were exactly right for who she was, mermaid or woman, and that as impractical and outrageous as it might be, he had no intention of letting her go any time soon.

This catch was a keeper.

She smiled again, and his heart leaped high in his throat. She bit her pink bottom lip, looked faintly guilty, and then said, "I guess I got caught by the wrong fisherman. Obviously you're not Ken Bristol, the congressional candidate, and this isn't the good ship *Andrea*."

Mark almost said, *I'll run for Congress if you want me to*, but instead he said, "No, I'm Mark Forsythe."

Suddenly Jillian found herself thinking that if she had to get caught by anyone, she was glad it had been this man. Dressed in shorts and a skin-hugging T-shirt—the only garment, she thought, that shoulders like his deserved—he was deeply tanned with bright, intense blue eyes, and salt-and-pepper hair. Yes, she thought, looking more closely, his white-streaked hair was rich and thick and strangely at odds with his youthful face, dark brows, and lashes. He was the most gorgeous man she had ever seen. She wanted very badly to touch his hair just once, just to see if it felt as wonderful as it looked.

She held out her hand. "Hello, Mark. Thanks for rescuing me. Without my contact lenses, I guess the white blur I headed for was the barnacles rather than Ken Bristol's boat."

His large hand wrapped around hers, just as his smile wrapped around her, warmly. As she met his gaze, she knew it was more than his good looks that attracted her. She had a vague memory of those eyes looking into hers with compassion and caring and concern, and of those strong, brown arms lifting her and carrying her, holding her as if she were precious to him.

Tenderness from a man was something she had missed for so long in her life, and something in her, even in her semiconscious state, had responded to it strongly. There was a quality in his gaze that spoke to something deep inside her soul, as if they had known each other before in another life, as if he recognized the kinship they shared as much and as deeply as she did.

Oh, stop it, she told herself. She was being fanciful. It must have been from the bump on the head.

"Did you want to get caught by a certain fisherman?"

"Well, that was the plan. I mean, getting caught by a man named Ken Bristol was what I was getting paid for." She grimaced with consternation as she blurted out, "Darn! Now I guess I don't get paid." Suddenly she bit her lip and drew her brows together. "Oh, heavens! Robin! He's a diver. He'll be down there looking for me! Unless—did anyone see you bring me here?"

"I tried to make sure no one did," he said with a grin. "I intended to keep you all to myself, Mermaid."

"Sorry, but I have to let someone know where I am and what happened, or there'll be all sorts of repercussions. Could you go and tell them that I'm here? They could send the Zodiac ashore for me."

With a heavy sigh of reluctance, Mark got to his feet and said, "If I must, I must, but I'd rather keep you, Mermaid." They shared a smile before he strode away around the end of an impressively large old house.

Jillian leaned back on her elbows, letting the sun soak into her skin, feeling it warm her as she stared at the house.

Gray and weathered, it looked as if it had been sitting there for a hundred years or more, although the patio and pool, along with umbrellaed tables, lounge chairs, and other outdoor furniture, all spoke of modern tastes—and obvious wealth.

Mark returned very quickly, frowning. "The boat is gone," he said without preamble, shocking her upright. "No Zodiac, no diver, no cruiser. The bay is empty."

Two

Suddenly Jillian was shivering again in spite of warmth of the sun. "But . . . how could they do that? How could they leave me? Oh, gosh, maybe they didn't! Maybe they're searching for me. I need to get to a phone." Her eyes swept the pool area. "Is—"

"No, there's no phone jack out here," he said, knowing what she was about to ask. "But that's not a problem. Hang on, Mermaid," he added as he lifted her into his arms and stood.

Jillian wrapped her arms around his shoulders, feeling the strength of his arms, the heat of his skin, the rigid wall of his chest. He was a big, powerful man, and she could feel all that power as he strode with her along a flagstone path toward the house. She tilted her head back an inch, wanting to see his eyes, but all she could see was his profile—a straight nose, a square chin, one strangely small ear tucked in close to his head, and that thick hair she found so tempting. If she could just lift one hand two inches, sort of by accident, she could touch it. With great strength of will, she kept her fingers locked together behind his neck.

When her icy hands clasped at the back of his neck, Mark felt guilty. He should have taken her inside long before. As warm as the sun was, she needed more than its heat. She was chilled right through. What she needed was to get out of her costume and into some dry clothes. A picture of Jillian Lockstead out of her costume, not in dry clothes but in his warm bed flashed across his mind, and it shook him. Damn, but she was doing incredible things to him.

It was easier to carry her when she was conscious and able to cooperate, able to put her arms around him and help. At least in one way it was easier. In other ways, it was much more difficult, he thought as he felt his heart rate increase to a level an aerobics freak would have been proud of. His breathing was considerably faster as well, and he struggled to control it. Oh, Lord, she felt good in his arms, scales and all, and those little drying tendrils of hair tickled his neck in a manner that nearly knocked him out cold when she moved her head.

"I'm sorry," she said, noticing his distressed

breathing. "I know how heavy I am in this suit. Honestly, it's the tail, not me."

He flicked a quick glance into her eyes and smiled as he elbowed open a set of French doors. "Do all mermaids have fat tails?"

"I'm the only mermaid I know, but my tail is made of neoprene, and without built-in weights to give it negative buoyancy, I'd go around head down all the time and ruin the effect of a mermaid's effortless swimming."

"When you were fighting that slop out there, it didn't look so effortless," he said, as he sat her in a chair by a small table.

"It wasn't. That was tough. Oh, look, I'm still dripping. I'll ruin your carpet and chair."

"It's all right," he said. "Water won't hurt anything." Gesturing to the phone on the table, he left her, returning with a large, thick white terry robe that he held out for her to put her arms into. She leaned forward while he tucked it down around her back. He drew her wet hair out from inside the robe and rubbed it hard with a towel for a few moments. Then, wrapping the towel around her head turban-style, he crouched in front of her, rubbing her cold arms through the loose sleeves of the robe, listening without a qualm to her side of the conversation.

"Get hold of Robin," she had been saying when he came back. "Tell him we blew it. He hooked me up to the wrong lure." She was silent while someone else spoke, then she exploded into speech.

"What do you mean, he knows already? How does he know? And why didn't he . . . Bristol actually caught a *fish*?" She laughed, but her amusement was short-lived.

"Well, if they saw me carried ashore," she said sharply, "why didn't they come and get me? . . . Oh." She covered the phone for a moment and said to Mark, "You locked the gate, he says."

He nodded. "Sorry. It locks automatically, and I didn't know anyone had followed."

She explained this to her boss, and Mark watched her face as she listened for another minute or two, then saw weary resignation flood her eyes as she rolled them skyward. "Of course I understand Bristol's a busy man and has other commitments, but surely he could have hung around long enough to get me back aboard his boat. No, Jim, obviously I didn't hear them shouting. I guess I was unconscious. Of course I'm all right. I have a small cut on my head and the hook caught me in the chest, but it won't be a problem for long." There was a pause, and Mark's estimation of the "Jim" on the other end of the line went down a long way when Jillian said with the same weary resignation, "Yes, Jim, I'll be able to work tonight."

She listened for a few more moments. "Okay. That'll be fine," she said. "I don't know where I am, but hold on and I'll find out."

She turned her eyes up to her host and met his steady gaze.

Mark looked back at her and smiled. He knew

exactly where she was. She was with him, and they were at sea, and the boat was rocking dangerously.

Mark moved toward her. He was so close to reaching out to draw her into his arms again that he didn't know how he stopped himself in time. He wanted to embrace her, to keep her close to his body, to tell her, "This is where you are, Mermaid, and this is where you'll stay." But of course he couldn't. Instead, he said, "Don't bother asking anyone to send a car. I'll be happy to take you wherever you want to go."

"Oh, I . . ." she started to protest, but he shook his head.

"My place is . . . hard to find from the road."

She sensed he didn't want his address given out and remembered the wrought iron fence and the locked gate. The house exuded the impression of old wealth, and she didn't blame Mark Forsythe for wanting to protect his privacy. She nodded and took the towel off her head, shaking her hair loose. It would dry better unwrapped. Running her hands through its length to untangle it, she explained to her boss that she didn't need a ride, watching as Mark Forsythe walked outside with long, even strides to hang her wet towel over the back of a chair. In the sun, the white in his hair was so bright, she could barely look at it without squinting, but she managed somehow. His tanned skin rippled over hard, sinuous muscles. She easily could have spent the next sixty-nine years watching the man move, she thought, but then what Jim was saying began to get through to her bemused brain.

Only it made no sense at all.

"Do it all over again?" she said with a gasp when she realized what he was asking of her. "Not on your life! That was a one-time-only shot, Jim. I don't care what it cost to hire the photographers! No! I'm not going down there again! . . . Then let Bristol use the film of himself playing the salmon, and they can splice in film of me in the tank . . . I don't care what they're willing to pay. Once was enough . . . No, I *didn't* like it," she snapped. "In fact, I hated it. I was scared and cold, and it wasn't the piece of cake you and Robin assured me it would be . . . Of course Robin wasn't cold! He was wearing a wetsuit! It was also a whole lot different from working in the tank. Buddy-breathing is for the birds."

There was a pause, and as Mark came back into the room, he could hear the sounds but not the words of a male voice arguing. "Well, then, it's for the fish," said Jillian. "Or the porpoises or whatever, or strictly for emergencies. It is not for me. Not again. Sorry, but if you want publicity photographs for any more political hopefuls, you find yourself another mermaid."

After another pause she said, "Yes, I'm just as committed to cleaning up the oceans as I ever was, and I believe that if he's elected, Ken Bristol would stand a chance of making some progress, but there has to be another way I can do my bit. I . . ."

She listened for a moment or two, and Mark noticed how pale she was again. He tucked the robe around her more tightly, and she smiled at him in thanks as she said softly but firmly, "I said no, Jim. And I meant it. Not again, not for any amount of money."

Mark heard her make a soft, dismayed sound and saw her stiffen, saw her eyes widen and her face go even whiter. He kept his hands on her waist, aware of the thick rubber suit between her skin and his but also very much aware of her female shape.

"You both told me it was an extra! That it had nothing to do with my regular job. And if you try to pull anything, changing my job description in the middle of the season, let me tell you, you won't get away with it. I'm the mermaid in the club, and that's that. Any extracurricular mermaiding you want done from here on out, you hire yourself another mermaid!" She hung up, and still staring wide-eyed and frightened into Mark's face, she wrapped her arms around herself tightly.

"Oh, brother," she said. "Can I do that?" Without waiting for him to reply, she went on. "But I did, didn't I? I as good as told my boss to get lost."

He stood and went to an intercom switch near the door. "Edward, could I have coffee for two in my den, please?" He thumbed the switch closed and came to sit opposite Jillian, drawing his chair up so close that his knees almost touched her thigh.

She could smell the scent of his soap, or after-shave, or shampoo, or maybe it was just him. It smelled good and male and comforting, and his voice when he spoke was deep and masculine and soothing. Well, maybe not soothing, since it made her heart beat fast, but it was . . . oh, she didn't know. She certainly did enjoy the sound of it. It had a rumble so deep, she almost could feel it. It made her want to lay her palm on his chest to see if she could feel the vibrations.

'Why don't you get out of that costume, Jillian? I could find you someth—"

"No!" Her sharp, almost panicked word cut him off, and he waved a hand as if to calm her.

"All right, all right. It was only a thought." Maybe she needed help getting out of it and didn't have anything on underneath. The thought made his breath catch in his throat.

"I . . . Sorry, I didn't mean to yell at you. But I'm fine like this. I'd rather keep it on, and really, I'd rather have someone else come and get me. I hate to bother you, and I'd make sure they were discreet about where you live and . . ."

"Jillian, I said I'd take you home. It's no bother at all."

"Thank you. I'm grateful. It's just that if you're going to drive me home, it'll mean you'll have to carry me to the car. . . ." The thought of being lifted into those muscular arms of his again, being held against that solid, warm chest was almost too much for her. Weakly, she forced herself to go on. "So maybe it would be better if . . ."

She let the sentence trail off as he shook his head. "I'll drive you home, and I'll be happy to carry you to the car," he said. In fact, he thought, he'd be happy to carry his mermaid in his arms for the rest of the day. Or maybe even the week. Hell, why not go whole hog? What about the rest of his life?

The thought slammed into his brain, and he shook his head. It was one thing to be so damned sexually aroused by the woman that he could hardly keep his hands off her, but it was entirely another to be thinking in terms of the rest of his life.

"How . . . how in the world did you ever get to be a mermaid?" he asked quickly, making conversation to occupy his mind because he felt as if he were on the verge of tilting into insanity once more. "That has to be the most unusual occupation I've ever heard of. And how long have you been doing it? Where?"

"Just for the past two years, in a place called the Pearldiver's Club. I did a lot of water ballet when I was younger and was on a synchronized swimming team," she said, "not that I ever expected it to be anything but a sport, but when I wanted a change from my regular job, my former training was what got it for me."

"Your regular job?"

"I'm a . . . I was a teacher."

"What kind of a teacher?"

"I was a guidance counselor and taught phys ed." She bit her lip, then said with a wry smile, "If I've lost my mermaiding job, I guess I'll have to go back to teaching."

Mark got the impression she was of two minds about it and wondered why. He smiled. "If you're as good a teacher as you are a mermaid, I don't see why there'd be any problem."

"I'll never go back."

He leaned forward slightly. "Why not?" he asked, as if it really mattered. "Didn't you like teaching?"

Suddenly she had the most absurd impulse to move closer and bury her face against the warmth she knew she'd find between his muscular shoulder and his strong neck, to feel his arms encircle her, hold her again, make her feel secure and unafraid. Instead, she leaned back and pulled the robe more closely around herself, pulling her tail in as tightly to the front of the chair as she could, telling herself that she could take care of her own life and didn't need to lean on anyone.

"I loved teaching," she said. "It's the most rewarding job in the world."

He raised his dark brows. "But you left it? Why?"

"Oh, I decided I needed a break," she said with a bright smile that he didn't believe for a minute. But he did believe that she had loved teaching. "I'd been at it for more than ten years, and it was time for something new. I've done some tutoring on the side these past two years, just to keep my hand in."

He was surprised at how long she'd been a teacher. It had been twelve years since she'd graduated from college, counting the two she'd been out of the teaching business, he calculated. He'd guessed her age to be around thirty. Now he upgraded that by three, maybe four years. And in spite of the bright smile that curved her pink mouth, something bleak in her tone and pained in her eyes told him there was a lot more to her choice to leave teaching than just having "decided" to take a break. He wondered if something had gone wrong with her job, and she'd been forced out of it.

"Where were you teaching, Jillian?"

"In Seattle. In a school downtown." Her eyes still seemed to smile, but he thought he saw sorrow in their depths. "Downtown" was an ambiguous word that could mean a lot of things, but coupled with teaching, it normally meant "inner city," and inner city could mean tough kids, knives, drugs, danger, constantly having to be on the alert, constantly having to be on edge.

Burnout? No, probably not, he decided, not when her eyes lit up and looked the way they did when she spoke of her former job. Yet there was sadness about her that suggested she hadn't left teaching of her own free will.

"What about another district?" he suggested.

"Did you try to find a position in a school up this way?"

She gave him a faint smile. "No," she said, amazed at the intensity of his gaze. With those blue eyes of his fixed on her face, it was as if he could read all the conflicting emotions that ran through her whenever she thought about what she'd like to do with her life, whenever she remembered the plans she had made and how circumstances had changed them. With anyone else, she would have looked away, hidden her feelings, kept herself private as she always did, but somehow his knowing she felt sad about having left the school system didn't seem to threaten her. She was comfortable with it and with him.

She wondered if she would feel as comfortable if Mark actually knew why she had left and suspected she would not. That was something she hadn't been able to deal with yet, at least not adequately, and she doubted that she ever would, which made meeting a man like Mark Forsythe doubly difficult. Because as attracted as she was to him, and even though he had a smile that warmed her right down deep inside, she didn't think she could let their relationship go any farther than it already had, which was nowhere at all.

"Who do you tutor and in what subject?" he asked.

"Mostly high school kids who are having trouble. Some math and remedial English plus college-level science for a university junior who was forced out for a semester due to illness."

His smile deepened. "All that and mermaiding too. What else do you do?"

"Not a lot, I admit. There isn't time for much more. I also have a d—"

She broke off when a tall, lean man with a gray mustache and a military bearing came in carrying a tray with a pot of coffee and slices of what looked like banana bread spread with butter and served on fine china.

He set the tray down and looked impassively at Jillian's tail hanging out from beneath the edge of the robe. Only his rapidly blinking eyes betrayed any surprise he might be feeling.

"I understood you were intending to catch a *salmon* for dinner, Mr. Mark," he said with a hint of an English accent. "Shall I thaw steak instead?"

Mark laughed and nodded. "Good idea, Edward. This is Ms. Lockstead."

"Miss Lockstead." Edward gave a little bow and left. Mark poured out two cups of coffee from the large china pot.

"Sugar? Milk?"

Smiling, she said, "Just the way it comes out of the pot, thanks." She couldn't help laughing softly. "He acted as if you had a mermaid in for coffee every morning of your life."

"Edward is British. He prides himself on being unflappable." Mark passed her the cup, and she balanced her saucer on her lap.

He looked more closely at the tail draping across the carpet. Now that it was dry, he could see that it was made of rubber, and despite how carefully it had been crafted to give the impression of scaled fish skin, he felt extraordinarily foolish again for having believed the illusion for so long.

He frowned. Why had he been so ready to believe that she was a mermaid? How much of his belief had been wishful thinking? Too much, he decided, because of course he knew better than to believe in magic, no matter how convincing the circumstances. He'd been taught by the age of four that Santa Claus and the Easter Bunny were really Mom and Dad, that Let's Pretend was just a game, and that Peter Pan couldn't really fly. So what had gotten into him when he gathered Jillian up out of the water and felt magic touch his soul for the first time in all of his forty years?

Looking at her again, he could feel the same light-headedness, the same bubbling happiness, the same suspension of disbelief.

Even in this now dimly lighted room, with its dark, masculine furniture, its book-lined walls and mullioned windows, there was a golden glow all around her, and sunlight in her eyes.

"Edward said you have something in here I should see." Jillian around at the sound of the young voice, and Mark paused in the act of reaching for the plate of banana bread.

A boy of perhaps ten or eleven came in. He had untidy brown hair, a sullen mouth, intense blue eyes, and darkly tanned skin. Jillian knew at once that he was Mark Forsythe's son.

He came to a halt, looking disgusted.

"A woman? Edward wanted me to see a woman?" he asked, and Jillian gave her tail a small kick, watching disdain fade from the boy's face to be replaced by disbelief, then total enchantment. He looked as if the tooth fairy had come to sit on his thumb, or as if a unicorn had just danced across the lawn.

"This is my son Christopher," Mark said, hiding his surprise at the boy's appearance. Edward must have been very persuasive in order to have gotten Chris to enter the same room as Mark. "Chris, this is Jillian Lockstead."

"M-mermaids have names?"

"Hello, Chris," Jillian said with a warm smile. "I'm afraid Edward was teasing you. I'm not really a mermaid. This is my costume. Your dad was good enough to help me when I ran into some trouble this morning trying to make a film out there in the bay."

Chris came farther into the room, perched on the edge of a chair near her, and continued to stare not at Jillian's tail but at her face.

"Are you a movie star?"

"Heavens no," she said. "Not even a TV star, although the film we were trying to make was for a TV commercial."

"You're pretty enough to be a movie star," he said, his blue eyes still wide and his mouth slightly agape. He looked intrigued now, not sullen, and Mark was grateful to Edward for having sent Chris in. It was the most he'd heard the boy say all weekend.

"Thank you," Jillian said. "That's one of the nicest compliments I've ever had."

"And true," added Mark, suddenly feeling left out.

She smiled at him, making him go light-headed again as he noticed a tiny dimple appear at one side of her chin.

"Have some banana bread," he suggested quickly before the magic could overcome him completely and turn him into a blithering idiot. "It's pretty good."

"Yeah," said Chris. "It's the only thing Edward can cook that tastes like food."

Jillian accepted. "Thanks, I'd love some. That was quite a workout I had, and swimming always makes me hungry." She bit into a piece and chewed appreciatively. "It is good. And it certainly tastes like food." She looked puzzled as she asked, "Is Edward your cook?"

Mark shook his head. "He's the caretaker here. His late wife Bessie was a fine cook, and Edward tries, he really does. He uses all of her old recipes, but somehow it nearly always goes wrong. But I'd hate to hurt his feelings by telling him he's a lousy cook."

He offered her the plate once more, and she accepted, then saw Chris shake his head, looking at his father as if he were a stranger—the kind of stranger he'd been warned against. Jillian frowned. What was going on? There was a tension between the two that would have been evident even to someone who hadn't done a lot of counseling of students and their parents.

Mark set the plate down and said, "It doesn't matter that Edward can't cook. I'm not such a bad cook myself, so if I'm having guests, which isn't often, I do the cooking."

"How do you manage that without hurting his feelings?" Jillian asked, half her attention on the sullen little boy who sat perched on the edge of his chair as if undecided whether to stay or to go.

"I get him to make the dessert, and I cook out on the barbecue."

"Or go out somewhere," muttered Chris, but his father ignored him.

"Bessie was old-fashioned enough to believe that barbecuing is strictly a man's job, so when she was alive, that's what my father or I always did. Edward never wanted to learn to barbecue, thank goodness."

Jillian laughed. "Hey, I don't think that's so old-fashioned. I happen to agree. Unfortunately, I have a daughter who loves her hamburgers barbecued, so I find myself standing over a bed of hot coals more often than I stand over a hot stove, which I much prefer."

He saw her looking longingly at the last slice of banana bread. Very, very carefully so that his hand wouldn't shake, he passed her the plate. Very, very carefully so that his voice wouldn't shake, he said, "Doesn't your husband like to barbecue?"

With a half-guilty grin, she accepted his offering. "My husband died seven years ago, Mark, before Amber was born."

"I'm sorry."

"Don't be, please. It was a long time ago, and the pain has faded. I'm not lonely. I have Amber and my mother."

"My mother's dead," Chris said, looking down at his lap. He linked his hands together, and Jillian saw that he'd bitten his nails down almost to the point of drawing blood.

"I'm sorry, Chris," she said quietly, reaching out to touch those tense hands.

Chris flinched away from her touch. "She was killed in an accident last Christmas," he said, and transferred his gaze to his father's set face, adding softly but with such deadly malice that Jillian cringed inside, "Dad was driving."

Three

Mark shot to his feet and stood irresolute for a moment, his face white as he looked from his son to the door as if wondering whether to try to stop the words he knew must follow or whether to bolt. He chose the latter, striding to the patio where he stood gripping the rail that edged the top of the cliff. Even though he was far enough away that he appeared as little more than a blurred shape to her since she wasn't wearing her contact lenses, she knew his shoulders were so stiff and his neck was so rigid that his muscles must be aching from the tension as much as his heart must be aching from the animosity borne by his son.

She looked at the boy. "It was an accident, Chris."

He let a low, unchildlike, bitter laugh escape him as he glared at his father's back.

"*He* didn't even get a scratch. And all I got was a broken wrist."

For a moment Jillian was bereft of speech. Then she said gently, reaching out and taking Chris's stiff hands in her own, "I'm sorry, Chris. That was a terrible loss for you. And for your dad. It's good that you have each other."

Chris snatched his hands out from under hers and lifted his anguished, angry face. "Baloney!" he said emphatically. "Good that we have each other? Ha! You don't know what you're talking about, lady. For me it was a terrible loss, sure. That was my *mom* that got killed, you know. But for *him* it was exactly what he wanted. In one easy twist of the wheel he solved his biggest problem, but he didn't do it right. It should have been both me and my mom he killed, but he blew it and now he's stuck with me."

"Chris!" She wanted to argue with him, tell him he must be wrong, but recognized the futility of that.

"I'm sorry you're feeling so bad, Chris," she said gently. "You must miss your mom a lot, and feeling the way you do about your dad means you can't go to him for comfort. I wish I could help."

Her words seemed to surprise Chris. He darted a startled glance at her, and then rushed into an angry denial as if her compassion caused him even more pain.

"I am not feeling bad!" he cried, his face crumpling and his voice cracking even as he tried to control both. "I don't need you or anybody else to help me. I missed my mom for a while, but I don't anymore. I just don't want to have to live with a man who hates me!" He shot up from his chair and glared at her, defying her to argue. But even if she'd been so inclined, he gave her no chance to do it. Instead he spun around and tore from the room, crashing into the table where the coffee service stood. The china pot and one cup shattered against the leg of Jillian's chair as he slammed the door behind him.

Jillian bent at the waist and carefully began picking up what broken china she could reach, holding it in her hand, staring at the pieces as if she didn't know what to do with them. When she looked up, Mark was standing over her, and she felt as if he were just as shattered as the dishes his son had knocked to the floor.

"I'll take care of that," he said, and she set the pieces on the tray he held out for her. "Sit back and tuck your tail up if you can. There may be bits of china under it. Did you cut your fingers at all?"

"No," she said. "I was being careful." But she tucked her tail as much out of the way as she could while Mark picked up shards of china from the thick pile of the carpet. She was certain when he spoke that he was glad to be able to look at the floor rather than at her.

"I'm sorry you had to hear our family's problems," he said, dumping a handful of chips onto the tray. "It was rude of me to desert you like that and let Chris mouth off."

She smiled when he glanced up momentarily. "It's okay," she said. "I don't believe there's a family in existence that doesn't have some problems. And most of them seem to be able to work them out, given enough time and enough love."

He stood and looked at her for an instant and then startled her by reaching down and lifting her from her chair. He carried her out through the door into the warm sunshine by the pool.

His eyes were filled with pain and anger and bitterness. "I love my son very much," he said. "I just can't seem to make him believe that. Because he's right, I was driving when his mother was killed. And as he sees it, since I took from him the very person he loved most in his life, I must have done it because I hate him."

Jillian raised one hand and impulsively curved it around his jaw, her thumb touching the corner of his hard mouth. "Poor Chris. He's such an angry little boy. I'm glad you love him, Mark. I think in time he'll be glad of it too."

As he looked at her, his anger fading, and the pain and bitterness dwindling in the intense blue of his eyes, something deeper than compassion was stirred to life in her, and she shivered even inside the warmth of his thick terry robe.

He bent his head toward her, and she knew she

had to stop whatever might be going to happen, because whatever it was, she wasn't ready for it. Quickly she said, "Please I really have to get home now, but I think you should go to Chris. He needs you, Mark. Let me call someone to come and get me. There's only one problem, though. I still don't know where I am."

This time he did it. This time he couldn't stop himself. He set one foot on the front of a chair and rested her bottom against his leg. "Don't you, Mermaid? I'll tell you where you are. You're in my arms, and I desperately want to keep you here," he said raggedly, lowering his head to kiss her long and hard and deeply, feeling her fingers clutching the flesh of his shoulders. He didn't know if she was trying to cling to him or trying to push him away, and he sensed that she didn't know either. He only knew that he had to hold her, had to kiss her, and that he wanted never to have to stop.

Jillian felt his heart hammering against her breast, felt his arms tightening around her, and didn't even consider trying to resist. When his tongue brushed over her lips, she parted them, opening her mouth to him. She was awash with sensation, drinking in the taste of him, breathing in the scent of him, need growing inside her like a neglected plant given sudden nourishment. His lips were hard. His body was hard. His muscles flexed as he slid one arm lower around her waist, one hand rising up to clasp a handful of her hair.

Yet in spite of that hardness, in spite of the passion with which his mouth devoured hers, she felt the marvelous sensation of being engulfed with tenderness, and she knew she was responding to it far too wholeheartedly—and to his kiss as well.

"Mark . . ." She murmured his name as she put her hands around his face and lifted his mouth from hers. "Enough," she said. "Please. No more."

He was breathing hard as he lifted his head and gazed at her. "Jillian . . . I—" He broke off and placed her on the chair. He wouldn't, couldn't apologize for having kissed her, because she had kissed him back, had wanted it as much as he had. "Please. Don't go. If you'll just give me a few minutes—have some more coffee or something—while I see to Chris, then I'll take you home. Just . . . wait for me." His voice shook and his eyes pleaded with her.

She hesitated for only a moment, then nodded. What else could she do? Other than calling someone to get her when she didn't know where she was, her only alternative was somehow to make her way to the water and try to swim home. But he, of course, didn't realize that. And as she looked at him, saw the misery and the pleading in his blue eyes, something in her softened, and she smiled. "Of course, I'll wait."

As she watched him walk away, she thought that he was a man who would be well worth waiting for. Then she remembered and was caught up in a wash of sadness that was broken into only when she heard the sound of bare feet running toward her.

"Hi," she said to Chris as he came to a stop near her, looking wary. "Did you see your dad? I think he was looking for you."

"I doubt it. He hates the sight of me."

"Why do you say that?"

" 'Cause it's true." He glowered at her, and Jillian waited for him to go on. Instead he changed the subject entirely. "Can you really swim in that thing?"

"Yes. I do a show in a nightclub. I dive underwater and do a sort of ballet."

"How do you breathe?"

"There are little air hoses concealed all over the tank behind pieces of coral or rock or within clumps of seaweed. I just duck behind something every couple of minutes and take a breath. And sometimes I come out at the top of the tank to let the people on the upper floor have a look at a mermaid."

"Could you swim here? In the pool? I'd kind of like to have a look at a mermaid." He didn't look or sound quite so sullen now, and Jillian smiled.

"Sure. One private performance coming up, Mr. Forsythe." She shrugged out of Mark's bathrobe, slithered off the chair he had placed her on, slipped into the water, and headed for the bottom. With powerful pushes of her tail, she skimmed along just inches above the blue-painted concrete, then did a few loops and turns before shooting to the surface like a porpoise, spouting a jet of water from her mouth directly toward Chris's bare feet.

Chris laughed, obviously enthralled. "Do it again! Do some more!" Obligingly she dove.

Mark, hearing the sound of his son's laughter for the first time in more than half a year, stood inside the doorway of his den and gazed out at the boy who squatted by the side of the pool laughing at the cavorting mermaid. For several minutes he watched them. Jillian slopped water over Chris's lap as he dangled his legs into the pool, then encouraged him to enter the water with her. His hands were on Jillian's shoulders when Mark approached the end of the pool. She was giving him the fastest swim he had ever experienced. His eyes were squeezed shut, but he was laughing happily. When she said, "Going down!" he closed his mouth and dove with her, her long hair swirling around his head.

She didn't keep him down long but brought him back to the surface near the shallow end and said, "Okay, friend, that's enough. I'm beat." Neither one had noticed Mark standing a few feet away.

"Wow!" said Chris. "Thanks. That was great! I wish I could go to your nightclub."

"It'll be another few years before you can do that," she said, hitching herself up onto the deck. "And by then I'll be an old lady with gray hair. Nobody would want a gray-haired mermaid."

Chris looked at her with adoration. "I would,"

he said. "Besides you could dye your hair. My mom did." He looked at her sideways. "I lied. I still miss her a lot, you know."

"I do know, Chris," she said evenly. "But I know something else that you probably haven't realized yet. It gets easier as time passes. The days when you hurt so bad inside that you wanted to die, too, get farther and farther apart, and one day when you least expect it, you'll discover that the hurt isn't quite so big, that you can think about her and maybe even smile and remember the good times."

"Was it like that with you when your husband died?"

"Yes, it was. And when my dad died too."

"But you still miss them? You haven't forgotten them?"

"No, of course not. I'll never forget either of them, and I'll always love them. But that doesn't mean I can't love someone else, that it would be disloyal or something if I did."

"Oh." Chris fidgeted. "I've got a picture of my mom in my room, but sometimes I can't remember what she looked like unless I look at the picture. And then I don't know if she looked like that all the time or just some of the time. It scares me. I don't want to forget her."

"I understand. You won't forget her. I can promise you that. Maybe your dad has other pictures of her you could look at."

A look of disdain crossed his face, and he stood

up. "I doubt it. I'm goin' in. He's prob'ly forgotten that he was looking for me, and I know he's got to drive you home. Will you come back?"

Jillian hesitated. "I . . . don't think so, Chris." She held out a hand to him, and he took it. "But I enjoyed meeting you, and who knows, maybe someday you'll come into the Pearldiver's Club in Boundary Bay and see an old, gray-haired mermaid swimming in slow, sedate circles."

He giggled, then caught sight of his father. For a moment he stiffened, before turning and running away so fast that he sent water drops flying all over. Jillian turned around to look at Mark Forsythe's tortured face.

He wrapped her in his robe again and lifted her into his arms. As he stood, she put her arms around him in what she hoped would seem to be a casual manner, but there was no way either of them could pretend that the desire that had sparked between them during that kiss lay very far beneath the surface.

She shivered, a delightful little tingle of sensation moving down her spine, and she felt him tighten his arms around her as if he, too, had felt it.

But as he carried her across the patio, she felt a silent sigh rise up in his chest.

"I'm sorry about you and Chris," she said. "Kids so often hurt their parents, even nice kids, and I think your son is certainly that."

He strode along a flagstone path to where a

garage was secluded behind a tall hedge. On the apron in front of one of the two closed doors stood a pale green Mercedes sports coupe. After seating her and making sure her seat belt was securely fastened, he got in and started the quiet, powerful engine. Only when they had pulled away from the house did he comment on her statement.

"His good behavior, when it occurs, is no doing of mine. His bad behavior, on the other hand, is all my doing."

"He's been hurt a great deal," Jillian said. "It must be hard for both of you to cope with the death of his mother."

"Lorraine and I were divorced nine years ago. I'm not mourning her, but of course I'm sorry she's dead. I liked her. We were good friends. Yet I can't seem to convince Chris of that. I've told him over and over that I didn't want to kill his mother —or him."

Jillian didn't quite know what to say. She certainly had an opinion on the subject, but it wasn't her place to express it.

She thought it was possible that Chris wanted those denials his father kept giving him. And the only way to get them, was to continue making the accusations. She wondered how Chris would react if his father stopped arguing the point, stopped trying to convince him, and simply gave him permission to believe what he wanted. Because, she was sure, that would leave a door open for Chris to change his belief whenever he was ready to do so.

It was none of her business, however, and Mark Forsythe was a stranger who wouldn't thank her for interfering.

Yet again she experienced the sensation that the word "strangers" didn't apply to them. No, something in her made her feel as if she had known him forever, and she wanted very badly to renew that acquaintance. The kiss they had shared had only sharpened her longing. She sighed. If only it were possible.

But she knew it wasn't.

They had reached the end of the long, twisting drive that led from Mark's house to the highway. He paused, looking at her quizzically.

"Where to, Jillian?"

"I live in Point Roberts," she said, naming the busy resort community just across Boundary Bay. The town was accessible on land only by crossing the Canadian border into British Columbia and then recrossing onto the little American peninsula that jutted down from the forty-ninth parallel. "The freeway's the best way to get there. At least it's the quickest."

"Do we need to take the quickest route?"

She hesitated for only a moment and then nodded regretfully. "I'm afraid so. I have appointments this afternoon."

As the car shot ahead at highway speed, her hair went flying around her face, whipping forward and back as the wind played with it. It felt nice to have it blowing around. It made her feel free and young and untroubled, as if she were twenty again, not thirty-four, and had no weight of responsibilities on her shoulders. Mark complied in silence with her instructions, and as they entered the flow of freeway traffic she saw him glance at her.

Feeling foolish, she quickly gathered her hair up in her fist and held it back. But he took her hand and turned her flowing mane loose, laughing with her as it flew around her face and neck, catching in her lashes, fluttering and dancing like pale, golden flames.

She watched his big, square, competent hands on the wheel. He drove as if the action were second nature to him. She didn't think he was the kind of man who ever drove carelessly or would have been responsible for an accident through inattention or recklessness. Although she knew even the best drivers could be involved in accidents, she also knew that they weren't usually the cause of them.

With uncanny accuracy, Mark picked right up on her thoughts. As he stopped at the end of the line of traffic waiting to cross through customs, he said, "You seem pretty relaxed in the car with me. Doesn't it make you nervous to know that I was the driver in a fatal accident?"

"I don't suppose you were at fault," she said.

"The police investigation said I wasn't, but try to tell that to Chris."

"You don't have to accept your son's evaluation

of it any more than you have to accept his judg-
ment that you deliberately killed his mother," she
said firmly.

"How do you know I didn't wipe Lorraine out on
purpose? It wouldn't be the first time something
like that had happened." He moved the car ahead
a few feet.

Jillian laughed softly. "You and Chris must be
very much alike. You're both grieving and looking
for someone to blame. He's blaming you, and you,
in taking that blame, are letting him give you the
punishment you think you deserve."

Mark flicked her another quick glance, and she
saw that his face had softened, his eyes lightened.
He smiled wryly. "Are you sure you're a teacher,
not a psychologist?"

She gave the question a serious answer. "As I
said, I was a guidance counselor. In order to get
that job I had to take several psychology courses.
But I'm no doctor, believe me. Whenever I ran into
something I couldn't handle on my own, which
was often, I referred the child and/or his parents
to a professional. I'm certain Chris's doctor knows
a lot more about how to help him than I do." It
was almost a question, and Mark shrugged.

"He's been getting help for more than six months,
but I haven't seen any progress. Sometimes I think
maybe I should let him do what he wants—live
with Lorraine's parents. But I keep hoping we can
make it, the two of us. We used to be so close."

"You will be again," she said quietly but with

great confidence. "Grieving can take so many forms. Chris is dealing with his through anger. Just go on loving him, Mark. It's all you can do."

With the car stopped once more, he turned to her and saw the deep compassion in her eyes. He suddenly was rocked by the urge to lean over, clamp his hand to the back of her head, and kiss her again until traffic behind them was backed up for a mile—or ten.

The attraction he felt for her was getting too far out of hand, he thought, feeling lost in the depths of her sea-green eyes. Her tangled, windblown hair caressed her cheeks. It made his fingers itch to do the same. He fought down the impulse. He had enough troubles right now without adding attraction to a woman to the list—especially not to a part-time mermaid who was so beautiful, she probably had more men begging to be let into her life than he had any chance of competing with. Besides, what woman in her right mind would be interested in a man who had a son whose needs were going to have to come first for a long, long time?

Nope. If he were looking for a woman—which he wasn't—he'd be looking for a good-time lady who could cheer him up when he needed to be cheered up and would disappear when he needed her to. And no matter what else Jillian Lockstead, mermaid, might be, he didn't think she'd qualify as a good-time lady.

Someone behind him honked, and he reluctantly drove on through customs and over the border. The drive from there to Point Roberts was made in silence.

Finally Jillian said, "Turn left at the next corner, then go straight ahead for six blocks." A few minutes later she spoke again into the silence. "It's the gray house halfway down the block on the right—there. You can park in the driveway behind my mother's car. I don't think she plans on going anywhere for a while, and you're still stuck with toting me around until I've changed out of this suit."

He pulled to a stop and asked, "Do you have a car?"

"Yes, but it's at the club. I went there to get my costume before this morning's little expedition."

"After you change, could I drive you there to get it? Or come later and take you to work?"

Briefly Jillian thought of arriving at work in his pale green Mercedes. It would be nighttime and he'd have the top up and it would be cozy and intimate inside the little car and . . .

"No, but thanks just the same. Robin, the diver who was with me this morning and supplied my air, is picking me up later."

He nodded and got out of the car, wondering if Robin was more to her than just a source of air. As he lifted her out he said, "I could get to like this." His breath stirred her hair as they crossed the driveway and he walked up the creaking steps to the porch.

The house had been built during the same era as his had, but there the similarity ended. More than just the ten or twelve miles of water across Boundary Bay separated their homes—and their lives.

She thought of the rolling green lawns she had seen beside Mark's shaded, twisting driveway, of the tall, stately cedar trees, the fence surrounding his property, of the remote-controlled gates at the entrance, and of the attractive lamps that seemed to be required security lighting. She wondered what he thought of her neighborhood which, with its droopy fences, unkempt lawns, and littered vacant lots showed its rapid decline.

It was a neighborhood she should move her family out of. But her mother had come there as a bride, had raised her three children there, and had spread her husband's ashes under the cherry tree he had planted there the day they had learned Jillian, their eldest, was on the way. She thought her mother probably would be as easy to transplant as that now-huge cherry tree.

She leaned over and opened the door, putting a smile on her face as she saw her mother coming from the kitchen. Quickly she introduced Mark.

"Mom, this is Mark Forsythe. He rescued me this morning when I got caught on the wrong fishing line."

Her mother raised her eyebrows and gave Mark an approving look. "That was fortunate." Then, coming closer, she said, "Oh, Jilly, you're hurt.

What a bump! And you're bandaged. You have a cut? Is it bad?"

"No. Just a little scrape. Mark, meet my mother, Shirley Elliot. And this," she said, as a little, dark-haired girl came to stand quietly beside her mother, "is my daughter Amber. Amber, this is Mr. Forsythe."

"Hello," he said to the little girl who didn't reply but only stood there with her dark green eyes fixed on his face, studying him. She apparently came to some favorable conclusion, because she replied to his greeting and smiled. When she smiled, her dark green eyes danced like her mother's sea-green ones, and then she laughed.

"Mom, you look funny! Mermaids don't wear housecoats."

Jillian laughed, too, embarrassed as she realized that Mark was still holding her in his arms. "Honey, open my bedroom door for us, please, so Mr. Forsythe can put me down."

Amber paused with a worried look on her face. "Did you break your leg again?"

"No, but it's kind of hard to walk on the tip of my tail," Jillian replied, making Amber giggle as she ran to swing open one of the doors off the short hall on the far side of the living room.

"There you go, Mr. Mark."

"Just Mark," he said at the same time as Jillian said, "Mr. Forsythe."

Amber swung open the door to a room in which there was a single bed with a bright gold spread, one chair, a tall chest of drawers, and a neat dresser with only a double picture frame on it. One side of the frame held her wedding photograph and the other a picture of a plump baby cuddling a kitten. Through a half-open closet door he could see a rainbow of garments on hangers and realized that she favored bright colors. Her closet was full of reds, hot pinks, and brilliant blues and greens, even a couple of shades of purple. Pairs of shoes were stored neatly in a rack on the floor of the closet.

He liked the almost austere tidiness of her room, and the smell of it was distinctly feminine.

"Mark, if you'll just put me down on the side of my bed, I'll be able to give you back your robe so we won't have to keep you any longer," Jillian said with a smile.

Reluctantly he did as she asked, and winked at her daughter who still stood by the open door, gazing up at him.

"Did you catch my mom on your fishing line, Mr. Forsythe-Mark?"

"Just Mark," he said again.

"Just Mr. Forsythe," Jillian said firmly. "And I'll explain it all later."

Shirley laughed. "I just made some fresh coffee, Mark. If you'll join us, you and Jilly can fight in comfort about what Amber will call you."

Her mother seemed, Jillian thought, to think that Mark was going to become an established visitor to their home, and that it would matter what Amber called him.

Quickly she set out to disabuse her of the notion.

"Mom, Mark just came in so I could change and give him back his robe," she said firmly. "His son is waiting for him at home."

"Thanks," said Mark, stepping out of her bedroom. "I'd love some coffee, Mrs. Elliot. It smells great."

"Those are cinnamon rolls you smell," said Shirley. "They're just about cool enough to touch, so please stay and share them with us. You should have brought your son. I've never known a little boy who didn't like cinnamon rolls."

As Jillian leaned over to close her bedroom door, she heard Mark laugh. "Or a big one. You couldn't beat me off with a baseball bat, Mrs. Elliot. Thank you. I'll stay."

Four

"Oh, heavens, call me Shirley. And sit down. You're too tall to be hovering in the doorway like that," her mother said.

Jillian heard the weak springs of the couch squeak as Mark sat down. She cringed, hoping he hadn't sat on the one that poked up uncomfortably into the tender anatomy of anyone unlucky enough to get that end of the sofa. She could hear the low rumble of his voice, her mother's higher tones, and then a delighted giggle from her daughter. So she wasn't the only woman charmed by Mark Forsythe.

Of course she wasn't. A man like him wouldn't lack for female companionship, and he said he'd been divorced for years. She wondered why he had never remarried. *Because he never wanted to, of course, dummy,* she told herself quickly. And most likely he'd never needed to. What was that about his not needing a good cook because he ate out a lot? She was quite sure that when he did dine out, he wasn't alone.

Sighing, she shucked his robe, holding it for a moment to her cheek, convinced she could smell the faint scent of his body on it. But of course she couldn't. It had been pristinely clean when he'd wrapped her in it. It hadn't been the one he'd worn when he got out of bed that morning. For an instant she toyed with the image of his large frame arising from his bed. Did he have hair on his chest? She glanced at the pure white of the robe in her hands.

Was his body hair sprinkled with white as the hair on his head was? Or was it all dark like his eyebrows and lashes? she wondered. What in the world was she doing, sitting there speculating about the body hair of a perfect stranger? Even one who had kissed her absolutely dizzy?

With a sigh, she draped the robe over the end of her bed and stripped out of her costume and the black bathing suit she wore under it. Her shower took only five minutes, and she wrapped her hair in a towel before drying herself off and dressing. She put on a hot-pink jumpsuit with a broad white belt, then shoes and socks, and, still tur-baned with the towel, she carried his robe out to him.

He was sitting on the shabby sofa, looking as

relaxed and as at home as he might have looked seated on one of the rich leather couches in his own den. Amber was on his knee, and together they were looking at one of her favorite books. In the kitchen Shirley was working on the cinnamon rolls, transferring some of them from the cooling rack to a plate. Mark's eyes were cast downward, but as if he sensed Jillian's presence, he lifted them and looked at her, smiling. Sitting Amber on the couch beside him, he stood up and came to Jillian.

"You're just a little bit of a thing without that long tail, aren't you?"

"Five three is just a tad below average," she said, feeling breathless with him standing so close. She supposed to someone over six feet, she would look like a little bit of a thing.

"I don't think there's a lot about you that's below average, Mermaid," he said quietly, his gaze sweeping from the top of her turbaned head down over her pink jumpsuit to the tips of her pink sneakers. Jillian's insides did flips and dives as she met his admiring gaze, but she knew she had to break this spell he was casting over her. Quickly she turned to speak to her daughter to explain how she had been caught on the wrong line. But Amber, with the attention span of most six-year-olds, hopped off the couch, dropping her picture book to the floor, and ran to the back door in response to another child's call.

"Billy and I are building a fort," she said just as the screen door slammed.

"Your robe. And thanks," said Jillian, handing it to him. He dropped it onto the couch.

"Coffee's ready," Shirley said, setting a cream pitcher in the middle of the table beside the sugar bowl and turning to busy herself pouring out three cups of coffee. She carried two of the hot rolls outside, and Jillian heard her call the children.

As Mark took a seat at the kitchen table, Jillian couldn't help remembering how he'd simply rung for coffee and had Edward bring it to where he was. He didn't seem to mind the way things were done here, though, and she felt a small warmth begin to grow inside her. As if he were feeling it, too, he smiled at her.

"I'd really like you to come back to my place and share that steak with me tonight," he said quietly, "or we could go out for dinner somewhere."

She met his gaze. Thinking of dressing up in something pretty, of sitting across a table from him, of the way he'd look dressed formally, made her stomach flutter madly and her heart leap wildly. How long had it been since she'd gone out to dinner with a man like Mark Forsythe?

The fact of the matter was that she had never gone out for dinner with a man like him, because he was one of a kind.

The trouble was he was not *her* kind. And if she did go out for dinner with him, she wouldn't know what to wear. She didn't think she had anything that would be suitable for the places he'd want to go. And as for going to his place . . .

She liked him too well, and she didn't think she could handle what would ultimately happen between them if they started dating. It had been more than two years, and there still was one hurdle she had yet to cross. Sometimes she had wondered if she would ever be able to cross it. But it hadn't become an issue. Not until now. And now it would only become one if she let it. Yet looking at him, she felt cold, icy fear creep through her, and she shivered. With Mark Forsythe, it could very easily become a terribly important issue.

"I'm sorry. That's not possible. I have to work tonight." In truth her first show didn't start until nine o'clock. She would have had plenty of time for an early dinner before work, but . . .

"Then lunch," he insisted, just as quietly.

Again she shook her head and sipped her coffee.

Her mother returned to the table and set down a plate of steaming rolls and pushed it close to Mark, who helped himself to one and then broke off a morsel, blowing on it to cool it before he put it into his mouth. It was delicious, but nowhere near as delicious as Jillian Lockstead's lips had been.

"Please?" he said softly, and then went very still inside, wondering why he was pleading with her. He had never done such a thing before. He frowned and looked down at the cinnamon-covered raisins that had fallen to the plate before him. Then he glanced warily at Jillian, wishing he knew where the mermaid-magic ended and the man-woman attraction began. Dammit, he didn't believe in magic any more than he believed in mermaids! But the attraction just wouldn't quit.

"I have three math students coming in"—she glanced at the clock on the control panel of the stove—"forty-five minutes."

He took another bite of the cinnamon roll, looking as if he had been transported to heaven, then swallowed. He'd thought he was going to compliment Shirley on her cooking, when he heard himself say, "Then what about a late dinner? When you get off work?"

She smiled. "On weekends, I don't finish my last show until one-fifteen. By the time I've showered and changed and driven home, it's usually after two and much too late for dinner. But thanks anyway. It was nice of you to ask me."

This time, to his relief, he managed to get himself under control. He shrugged and said easily, "Another time, then," and stood to leave.

Jillian realized that of course he didn't really care if she went to dinner with him or not. There must be hundreds of women who could and would and wanted to. And when it came to the last— those wanting to—she was certainly right up there among the most eager. She wished she hadn't had to turn him down.

•   •   •

Jillian found that Mark was constantly on her mind as the afternoon progressed, and she had to force herself to concentrate on her students as well as the needs of her daughter. He seemed to accompany her as she drove to work that night with Robin. But as she prepared to slip into the top of the huge tank in the Pearldiver's Club, ready to make her entrance from within the concealing fronds of kelp, she finally managed to clear her mind of anything and everything that a mermaid wouldn't think about.

Taking a deep breath, she lowered herself into the tepid water, entering another world.

Mark had never been to the club before. He sat at a table on the second tier that surrounded the massive tank, the focal point of the Pearldiver's Club, and took in the lush aquatic growth planted in the big saltwater aquarium. Huge, waving fronds of seaweed, green, red, brown, and gold, grew from coral-encrusted rocks and what might have been the hull of a sunken pirate ship.

Vibrantly colored schools of tropical fish darted in concert between fans of pink, white, black, and orange coral, as if moved by a single mind, swinging through the beams of waving spotlights. Shells lay here and there—large, spiked ones with opalescent, peachy insides; small, delicate ones shaped like long spirals in white and gray and coal-black, and even a couple of brilliant yellow ones.

An ornate jeweled tiara of blue and white stones hung from a coral branch, and a pewter loving cup stood half-buried in white sand near the center of the bottom of the tank beside a tilted brass chest, which had strings of pearls spilling forth, along with rings and bracelets and necklaces of rubies, sapphires, and diamonds. The gleam of gold and the glow of emeralds glittered within its depths, and glinting silver coins were scattered all around.

A moving spotlight followed one school of fish, then switched to another. Slowly, the houselights began to dim. From somewhere in the recesses of the darkening club, a slow drumroll began then built, as the lights in the tank slowly brightened until it was a vast, green glow within the darkness of the packed club.

All eyes were on it, all sound had stopped. She slowly came from behind a huge sheet of shiny brown seaweed with her hair floating behind her like a backlighted halo of gold. Wrapped around her head was a broad, sequined band that glittered with the same blue, green, and silver colors as her shapely body and tail, hiding from the world the fact that even a mermaid could bang her head on the rocks.

A collective sigh went up from the audience. The women all seemed to want to change places with her if even for only an hour, to have a chance to be the magic, ethereal creature she was, the stuff of fantasies, the stuff of dreams, the stuff of a thousand legends, cynosure of every eye. And the men seemed to yearn to be in that very authentic looking seascape with her, swimming effortlessly through the water as a bird would fly through the air. Each one seemed lost in a secret dream of capturing her, holding her in his arms while they rolled and twisted and cavorted together in the unreal realm where she seemed so at home.

But one, only one, sighed and smiled as he remembered exactly what it felt like to hold that mermaid in his arms.

Enchanted, he watched her, caught up in the beauty she created as she went from a rolling dive into a graceful soar, chasing the fine stream of bubbles that rose away from her, then abandoning them, letting them rise unheeded as she made for the bottom of her man-made ocean environment. She twisted sideways, and reached out a hand to the glass, touching the same spot where a red-faced, middle-aged man had placed his palm. She smiled, and her sea-green eyes shone as if she could see the admiration and longing in the man's face, but then she was gone, chasing a bright blue and gold fish as it darted for the cover of a mass of green fronds.

The mermaid, too, disappeared behind the greenery, only to reappear seconds later on a different tangent, bubbles still streaming in a fine silver trickle from her softly parted lips. Her tail flipped gracefully, and she did a complete loop, landing upside down against the wall where yet another lucky customer was treated to one of her glowing smiles and a fingertip pressed to the lips he pressed to the glass. Then she rose up, up, up, until all that was visible was the pale shimmer of her arms and hair, and then even that was gone, leaving only the swirl of her tail as she half-emerged from the water to let herself be seen by the customers seated on the mezzanine surrounding the top of the tank.

She stayed for some time, and then descended once more, swirling through the water with the ease of a porpoise. For half an hour she cavorted, her graceful sweeps and dives, her tantalizing disappearances into and reappearances from the swaying, living growth, holding her audience in thrall. Now and then, she would choose an article of jewelry from the treasure chest—a rope of pearls to adorn her graceful neck; a glittering ruby bracelet for one arm, a gleaming series of golden bangles for the other. A ruby hair clip arose with her, along with a silver-backed comb one of the times she left the water to sit at the top of the tank. When she returned to the depths, she was followed by a shower of coins and costume jewelry which she gathered in both hands and let fall into the treasure chest.

She teased the schools of tropical fish, chasing them with white, fluttering hands. Then, with tidbits she picked up from the bottom or plucked from coral fans growing out of encrusted rocks, she tempted them to come to her, as she tempted the club's clients to come close, closer to the glass.

Then, long before anyone had a chance to tire of her show, she was gone. The main lights in the tank were dimmed leaving only a few moving spots through which the exotic tropical fish swam to show off their vivid colors.

The music, of which Mark had been unaware, now changed from the floating, mesmerizing strains that had accompanied Jillian's show to an upbeat, louder tune over which applause rose and rose and then finally faded, leaving voices to grow loud and glasses to tinkle with ice once more as drinks were ordered with renewed enthusiasm and the houselights came up again.

People around him ordered more drinks and food, talked and laughed and enjoyed each other's company. He was even invited to join another table, the people seeming concerned that he was alone and not having any fun. He declined. He knew that only the day before he, too, would have preferred to have been part of a laughing group. Yet now, somehow, it didn't appeal to him. His gaze kept straying from his watch to the dimly lit tank, where the fish were now the main attraction, knowing that the next forty-five minutes were likely to be the longest he had ever spent.

When the drum roll came again and the houselights dimmed as the tank was illuminated, he held his breath, waiting. This time she didn't come seductively from behind a curtain of seaweed. Instead she burst forth in a cloud of bubbles from a cave in the rocks that he hadn't noticed before, her tail swirling, her arms stroking strongly, and she rose directly to the top of the tank.

Looking up, he could see that she had come out of the water, and as many others tried to do, he made a dash for the stairs. Being tall, his long strides carried him quickly to the mezzanine floor, but he was too late to find a place near the rail.

Still, over the heads of others he could see her. Sitting on a rock that projected from the water near the center of the tank, she stretched out an arm and filled a peach-colored shell with the clear, fresh water which came streaming down from a crag high above her small island. Filling it again and again, she rinsed her shoulders then her hair, trickling the water through its sleek pale gold. She drank deeply from the shell's lip before letting it fall, tumbling through the depths toward the bottom while she combed her long hair, now and then lifting her tail from the water and splashing her delighted audience. When a customer stood and withdrew a glittering piece of jewelry from his pocket, tossing it toward the mermaid, she caught it expertly and blew the donor a kiss. The audience exploded with applause, then she dove beneath the surface once more, and the applause rose to nearly deafen Mark as he made his way back down the stairs.

Once more at the lower level of her liquid stage, he saw her emerge from a group of coral fans and approach the glass to greet yet another grateful customer with an intangible touch of her fingertips to his lips. She reached out and caught another trinket dropped from somewhere above, smiled, and rose lazily to the surface, where he was certain she would blow a kiss to the bestower of the bejeweled bracelet she now wore around her right wrist.

Something inside him snapped, and he stood there, fighting fury as he watched her act come to an end. It was her last show of the evening, and he was certain he detected weariness in her wave just before she ducked into a crevice in the rocks and disappeared from view. At once, before the crowd had risen from their chairs, he turned on his heel to stride from the club.

He was sure he would never come back.

It was stupid. It was jealously. It was the most primitive emotion he had ever experienced, but he hated having his mermaid accept baubles from other men. Oh, hell, he was out of his mind! She wasn't his. He didn't want her to be his!

He got into his car, slammed the door, and leaned on the wheel. He shouldn't have come to the Pearldiver's Club. It wasn't his kind of place. He started the car and put it in gear, pulling out of the parking lot so fast, the tires squealed.

"Pearldiver's Club," he said scathingly to himself. "What a hokey name. What a stupid concept."

All those fantasizing, panting men gawking at Jillian, pressing their hands and faces to the tank's walls, pretending they could feel her touch through the glass. He had touched her skin with his own. He remembered its silk. He didn't have to fantasize. It was there, imprinted on his brain, indelible and burning.

He hated the remembered sensation even while he yearned for it again. He slowed, stopped at the side of the road for several minutes to think. Then he made an illegal U-turn, heading back the way he had come.

Jillian had seen Mark. She was certain of it. In spite of being without her contact lenses, she was positive he had been there. As she showered the salt from her tired, aching body, she wondered why there was no note from him in her dressing room. Wasn't that the way it was done? She knew it was. It had happened before, only all the other notes had been addressed simply to "The Mermaid," as if it was too much trouble for the man to find out her name. She'd often thought that perhaps the men who asked her for dates didn't want to spoil the fantasy by allowing her an identity other than Mermaid. Many of them had offered her money for personal appearances at stag parties or pool parties. A few even had offered her money for more than just that. It hurt her to feel that so many of her audience thought of her as nothing but a commodity. But maybe it went with the territory, and as long as she didn't feel like one herself, what other people thought hardly mattered.

Except for Ken Bristol, the congressional candidate, she had made it a point of refusing all and any offers. For one thing, she was much too tired after three shows on weeknights and four on Fridays and Saturdays to even consider going anywhere with anyone for any reason at all. She had agreed to the candidate's request because it had not come in the form of a note in her dressing room, but as a formal business proposition to her through her boss.

Yet in spite of her refusal to have a late dinner with Mark Forsythe, when she'd seen his distinctive, salt-and-pepper hair and tanned face in the crowd around the mezzanine, she had expected him to repeat his invitation. And she knew if he had, she would have accepted. No one ate dinner at two o'clock in the morning, however, a cup of coffee and some scrambled eggs would have been nice.

She sighed and hopped out of the shower, wrapping herself in a towel, and remembered that he hadn't taken his robe with him when he'd left her mother's house. It was now draped over the back of a chair in her bedroom. She blew her hair dry, dressed in jeans and a warm sweater, pulled on socks and sneakers, and grabbed up her purse.

Letting herself out the back door into the brightly

lighted parking lot, keys already in her hand, she unlocked her car, locked the door behind her as she closed it, and then started the engine. As she pulled out onto the street, she yawned.

Because of the publicity stunt that morning, she'd been up for nearly twenty hours and hadn't been able to sleep in as she usually did after her late stints at the club. She was thankful it was Sunday and no students would be coming. When she got up, if she wasn't too tired, she could take Amber on a long-promised picnic and get to bed again by nine. Sleep, she thought. Blessed sleep. There never seemed to be enough time for it, and she found herself yawning too frequently. Maybe she was just bored. Nightclub work, as well as it paid, certainly wasn't very mentally stimulating.

However, she definitely was feeling exhausted enough to be paranoid, she decided several minutes later, when, having made the three customary turns that would lead her home, she saw the same set of headlights behind her. They were exactly the same distance behind her as they had been when she first noticed them as she'd left the club's parking lot.

No matter. She was nearly home and would be safe inside in another thirty seconds. As she turned into the narrow driveway, the other car caught up to her. She shut off her headlights, keeping her doors closed and locked and watched the other vehicle slow to a crawl then stop across the street by the fence that surrounded a small park.

It was a large white car. An Oldsmobile, she thought, and this year's model. Not the kind of car normally driven by someone from her neighborhood, but the kind any of the club's customers might have driven—and a lot of other people as well. Had one of the customers followed her, or was it simply a coincidence that she had noticed it behind her as soon as she'd pulled out of the parking lot?

Quietly she opened her door and closed it, heading for the front porch. Of course she hadn't been followed. The other car had come the same way for reasons that had nothing to do with her. They were probably a couple of kids looking for a quiet place to do a little making out.

She smiled as she crossed the veranda and glanced across the street again. Yes, that was it. The headlights of the white car went off, but no one got out. She wondered for a moment what kind of parents would lend a kid a car of that caliber and not enforce a much earlier curfew.

Then, just as she unlocked the front door, a truck came around the corner, its headlights illuminating both sides of the road, and she couldn't help stealing another look at the car across the street. She froze as did the occupant who was staring at her, and even over the distance, now that her contacts were firmly in place, she recognized him at once.

Mark Forsythe! Her heart lurched inside her

chest and she stared for another second or two, wondering why?

Suddenly she had to know, but before she could even start across the street, he put the car in gear, turned on the lights, and was gone, leaving only the imprint of bright red taillights flashing green on her retinas as she closed her eyes.

Five

She dragged herself into bed and waited for sleep to come, but it eluded her for much too long as she relived the events of what had been a very long and very full day. Finally, just as the birds began to sing in the cherry tree, she slept. When she awoke it was midafternoon, and she could barely move. Amber, good little kid that she was, swallowed her disappointment about the postponed picnic and settled for hot dogs on a blanket in the backyard.

Monday Jillian felt a little better but still ached as if she had been pummeled which, she realized, she had—by waves and by being bashed into the rocks. She and her mother cleaned house, Jillian taking over the chores she felt were too heavy for the older woman, and Amber played outside in the yard with her friend Billy until they fought and Billy went home in a huff.

It was a normal Monday, Jillian thought, if Mondays were supposed to be blue. She hugged Amber to make her feel better, wishing she had someone to hug her and make her feel better too. Why she felt so down was a mystery to her.

It wasn't as though she had expected Mark to call or show up on Sunday. It wasn't that she was *really* disappointed that he hadn't made any attempt to talk to her after following her home on Saturday night. It was just . . . Darn it, she didn't know what it was, but she'd better get over it before she had to be back at work, smiling, cheerful, performing for a club full of guests who wouldn't expect a down-in-the-mouth mermaid.

By Tuesday she was fine and did her three shows with full enthusiasm and energy. It was in the water, under the water, that she felt best. There she was aware of no awkwardness, no lack of grace. There, she knew she was, to her audience, beautiful. She wondered if, when he had watched her last Saturday night, *he* had thought her beautiful.

As she showered and changed after work, she wondered if he had been in the audience. She had gazed as best she could into the crowd on the mezzanine, but unless he'd been fairly near the front, she knew she'd never have spotted him. Yet as she pulled out of the parking lot, a car followed her home, pausing half a block away as she got out of her car, went onto the porch, and unlocked the door. When she opened it again quickly after entering to peek out, the car was gone.

It hadn't been a green Mercedes nor had it been a white Oldsmobile. It had been a taxi, and it was there on Wednesday night, too, following her home like a faithful shepherd. She watched for the headlights again on Thursday, saw them following her and smiled, but when they turned into the driveway behind her, she realized that her taxi driver escort was not with her that night.

Mark was, in the Mercedes.

She opened her door and got out as he did the same, and they stood looking at each other in the dim light of the yellow bulb over the front door of the house.

"You followed me," she said softly, the statement clearly a question. "Last Saturday too. And you've had me followed home by a taxi ever since."

He nodded. "It's so late when you leave work. Do you always drive home alone?"

"Of course." She seemed surprised he would think otherwise.

"It's a dangerous practice, Mermaid. Cars can break down."

"Not mine," she said. "It may not look like much on the outside, but I'm careful to keep it well maintained." That was something she was always very careful of; women who worked late at night and traveled home alone had to be confident that their cars weren't prone to breakdowns.

It wasn't, however, good enough for him. "A tire could go flat."

"I've known how to change a tire since I was sixteen years old. My dad wouldn't let me get my license until I could."

"And what happens if some creep comes along when you're out of the car changing that tire?"

She smiled at the vehemence in his tone. It was touching. Nobody—nobody but her mother—worried about her. "If I'm changing a tire, I'm likely to have a lug wrench in my hand or at least nearby. But thank you for caring."

He didn't speak, just lifted a hand and brushed her hair back from her face, lightly stroking the healing cut on her temple. He remembered his first sight of her, the elation he'd felt as he gathered her up and held her out of the cold water, the magic, their kiss. He ached to repeat it but . . .

"You were—are—so beautiful, Jillian. Every man there tonight wanted you." She knew that meant he had been there, and her heart beat high in her throat even while she felt ill with disappointment. He was one of those men. One of the customers. One of the fantasizers. Only . . . wasn't it best for him to go on seeing her as a mystical being rather than a real woman, when the reality was so much less?

"I hated them all for their thoughts," he confessed. "Even though I was sharing their thoughts. What are you doing to me, Mermaid? With your magic, with your beauty? I'm supposed to be in town, but I hired someone to stay with Chris and drove up after work because I had to see you again."

She wondered if he was going to kiss her again, and if he did, what would it be like? She remembered the way his lips had felt—hard, almost bruising in their urgency—and deep inside her something grew hot and liquid. But fear rose up as she thought of trying to cope with the kind of relationship Mark Forsythe probably had in mind. Oh, who was she kidding? When she thought about a relationship with him, what he had in mind was exactly what she did too. But it wasn't to be.

But oh, how she wished it were otherwise.

"I had to see you again," he went on, breaking into her thoughts. "I had to see if you were real or if I had only imagined you and your incredible beauty."

"It . . . It's not real. It's only an act," she whispered. "A fantasy I create for my audience. And only there in my tank am I beautiful."

She wasn't asking for compliments. She knew her own limitations. She had a nice nose and mouth and an ordinary pair of eyebrows, but her eyelashes were much too pale. When she wasn't working she wore mascara, but even the most waterproof product she could find couldn't withstand the test she put it to each night, so she didn't wear it at work. She knew that without it, other than when she was in her mystical mermaid environment, her eyes looked almost lashless, unfinished, plain.

"You are beautiful in or out of the water, in or out of your costume." His voice was soft. His eyes held the same look they had when he had gazed upon her mermaid shape by his pool. He had wanted her then, too, even as realization dawned that the whole thing was a hoax. She had been aware of his wanting her, but she knew it was because he didn't know. He may have visualized her without her costume, but his vision was so terribly, horribly wrong.

He didn't even know what he was seeing now, as he looked at her, as he touched her. His hand as it slid down the side of her face to her neck was warm and ruggedly callused. His nails, she had noticed earlier, were neatly cut and were pale against his skin. He had nice hands. She liked the look of them. Even more, she liked the feel of them—on her.

"I want to see more of you," he said, and she shuddered at the thought, nearly weeping at the feeling that welled up in her.

Why? Why? Why?

She was certain he could feel the pulse hammering hard under the heel of his hand. How could he not be aware of it? How could he not be aware that his touch was the cause of her increased heart rate? She stepped back, wrapping her arms around herself, shaking her head. "No."

"I passed an all-night restaurant not far back,"

he said. "After all that work, aren't you even a little bit hungry? I remember your saying last week that swimming always makes you hungry. What about some bacon and eggs? Or a sandwich, or whatever?"

She smiled, remembering her thoughts in her dressing room the previous Saturday when she had expected—no, had yearned for—a note from him. Even while she knew she should turn, say good-night, and go inside, she said, "I was going to scramble some eggs myself. Would you like to join me?"

His wide grin was her reward as he took her hand and walked with her on tiptoe up the creaking steps to the even creakier porch. In the kitchen they whispered and laughed like giddy children as they made coffee, scrambled eggs, and buttered toast. Then, with their midnight feast piled on a tray, they went downstairs into what Jillian referred to as the rumpus room.

The term fit. The room was straight out of the sixties, complete with fake wood paneling on the lower two-thirds of the walls, cork on the upper third, and vinyl furniture under a low ceiling with acoustic tiling between darkened beams. Indirect lighting gave off a soft glow.

Mark laughed as he set the tray down on the table beside the coffeepot Jillian had put there, and said, "I love this room! It makes me feel like I'm in high school again, visiting a girlfriend and sneaking around hoping her father won't come down and order me out because it's past his daughter's bedtime."

Jillian put a tape in the cassette player, keeping the volume low so as not to disturb her mother and Amber, who were asleep upstairs. She smiled as she passed him a plate of eggs and toast and poured the coffee.

"Did you do a lot of that as a teenager?"

"What? Keep girls up past their bedtime?" He grinned, creases bracketing his mouth, fanning out from his eyes. "I guess I did my share of it. What about you? Did you ever have to have your boyfriend kicked out because it was too late?"

"Oh, frequently, at least until my dad came home one night when I thought he was already in and caught me on the living room sofa with a boy he didn't like. After that, I was a lot more careful, and besides, soon after I went away to college." She didn't add that her father had died of a massive and unexpected heart attack that same year.

Seated side by side on the couch, they ate until their plates were empty.

Sensing Mark's gaze on her, Jillian looked at him, trying to read what was in his eyes. Whatever it was, it spoke to something vital far down inside her soul, and it was asking questions for which she didn't think she had any answers.

When his hand reached out, large and capable, to cover hers, she turned hers under it and clasped her fingers around his. She turned his hand over and traced the hard calluses there with one fingertip.

"What do you do to get these?" she asked.

His glance flicked over her face almost shyly. "I build trucks."

"Really? What kind of trucks?"

"Logging trucks," he said.

"You own the company that builds them? You don't do it yourself, personally, do you?" she asked, thinking again of his "weekend cottage" and wondering what kind of house he had in the city. Mark Forsythe was no factory employee.

"Me, personally," he assured her, smiling. "I even provide the logs. I build fire trucks, too, with ladders and hoses and firemen, and pickup trucks with campers on the back, or canoes or dirt bikes, and moving vans with loads of assorted furniture in them, and houses to put the furniture into once it's delivered. Right now I'm working with a designer toward moving out into the world of boats. Ever heard of Elfshop Toys?"

"*Elfshop Toys!*" Of course she had heard of them. Everyone had. "You make those? Why, they're wonderful!"

"Do you think so?" He looked at her as if he thought she was wonderful, and the world slipped into slow gear for several minutes while she wondered again whether he was going to lean forward and kiss her.

He didn't.

She swallowed hard and said, "I really think so. I bought Amber one of the logging trucks for Christmas last year. She loves to spill the logs off and then scramble around finding them, stacking them up again and fastening the chains over them. I like wooden toys. They seem so . . . so much closer to nature—warmer—than plastic. I haven't seen the moving vans and houses yet though."

"They'll be on the market by Christmas, but there are a few prototypes ready now. Would you like a set for Amber?"

She thought of how much pleasure Amber would get out of a toy like that, but shook her head and said with a smile, "Thanks, but I'll wait and buy her one. When do you expect to have your boats in the water?"

"In time for next summer," he said, and went into an enthusiastic description of what they would be like. They both agreed that kids would love them.

"How did you become a toymaker?"

"My family owned a large logging operation. You may have heard of it," he said with a wry grin. "Corville-Forsythe."

He clasped her hand harder, and said sternly, "Now, you quit looking at me like that. None of it's my fault. I didn't earn any of the money C.F. makes. I simply inherited some of it." Before she could comment that inheriting even some of it put him in a financial bracket she couldn't even begin to imagine, he went on.

"When I was a teenager, my dad sent me out to a different logging camp every summer so that when I took over the business and had to deal with the workers, I'd have some idea of what they were doing and what problems they had. During one of those summers, an old fellow taught me to carve wooden animals, and I discovered a talent I never knew I had. Since then I've loved working with my hands making toys. After college, when I declined my father's offer to take an active part in the company, my dad and his partner, Jason Corville, who had no one to take over from him either, very sensibly decided to go public. When my dad passed away a few years ago, I inherited his half of the business. But fortunately for the stockholders, I didn't inherit the responsibility for running the company.

"Fortunately for me, too, as I'm able to indulge myself. I do what I want to do and that is make wooden toys. I have a small company in Seattle where I employ close to fifty people, and we all work together. As the market expands, we expand. We may not make a lot of profit, but we all like what we're doing."

"And that," she said softly, picking up her coffee to sip, "is very important, isn't it?"

For several minutes he didn't reply. He sensed her understanding of the grief he had experienced as well as caused in turning down the opportunity to take over his father's business, that it had hurt him deeply to disappoint the old man. Her compassion, he thought, would be equally shared between the two of them.

"Very important, Jillian," he said finally. "I know that very few people are given the options I was given, and don't think I'm not aware that it was my father's hard work which enables me to indulge myself the way I do running what almost amounts to a nonprofit organization."

She smiled. "I think I knew that without being told. Your work is important to you for more reasons than just your own personal happiness, isn't it?"

Her understanding touched him deeply. He wanted to gather her into his arms and hold her, to thank her for not judging him. So many people had considered him ungrateful and lacking in filial duties, but he thought what he was doing was as important in its own way as carrying on his father's empire would have been. There, in the quiet room with only faint background music and dim light surrounding them, he wanted to tell her about his company, about his workers, about the pride he felt in their every accomplishment. But he didn't want to appear boastful. It wasn't false modesty, though, that kept him quiet; even as he longed to be able to talk to her about it, he felt that the friendship between them was too tenuous yet, the building trust just a small, fledgling thing. And there had been those who'd scoffed, who'd assured him he was wasting not only his father's hard-earned money but his own precious time.

"Do you like what you're doing, Jillian?" he

asked, knowing he had to change the subject before he gave into his own impulse and spread all his hopes and dreams before her, babbling like a fool and asking for her approval.

She hesitated as he had done, and then said, "In many ways. It's not much of a mental challenge, I admit, but I do enjoy most of it."

"But you'd rather be back working in the school system."

It wasn't, she recognized a question.

"I did love teaching and counseling," she agreed carefully. "It's—it was—what I did best."

He looked at her over the rim of his mug as he drank another mouthful of coffee, then set the mug down, leaning back on the couch. Rolling his head sideways to look at her, he asked quietly, "Why did you leave it?" He knew he had asked her before, but her answer hadn't satisfied him. This time, in the quiet of the night, with the beginnings of an aura of trust wrapping around them, he thought he might get the truth.

But she, too, seemed to think that it was too soon for confidences. He found her answer evasive.

"There were several reasons. I got sick and had to come home for a while. When I was better, I discovered that I couldn't . . . handle . . . a full day in front of a class, so I did the next best thing, took the job at the club. Besides, just about then, my mother started suffering from angina attacks. The doctors said they weren't life-threatening, but I didn't—don't—want to leave her alone. And I do like my job at the club. Swimming was my avocation, as I said. I simply turned it into my vocation."

She smiled wryly. "Surprisingly, for a lot fewer hours and for work that requires no brains at all I'm earning nearly twice as much as I ever did in the classroom. I've always wondered why some football players earn more than most brain surgeons, and exotic dancers—mermaids included—more than teachers. It seems incongruous that people are so willing to pay to be entertained and so chary when it comes to the important issues like medicine and education."

"It doesn't seem fair, does it?" he said.

"No, but I must confess that the hours suit me and I like the extra pay. It's nice being home with Amber during the day. From the time she was only a couple of months old I've had to work. These past two years have been a real joy because I can spend so much more time with her. Of course, it'll be different starting in September when she's in school all day."

"You're going to miss her, I know," he said. She was sure he did know, this man who had been forced to live apart from his own child and who, even though he now had that child with him, was still far apart from him in all the ways that counted.

"Yes, I'll miss her like crazy, but it's something all parents have to go through, and it'll mean less strain on my mother. She likes to pretend she's just fine, but I worry about her.

"She needs a life of her own too. She's certainly

young enough to marry again if she had the chance to get out and meet people instead of being tied down with my child most evenings."

For a moment he was silent, looking down at his lap. He set his coffee cup down. Then, with a quick glance up at her, one she was beginning to think characteristic of him, he said, "And what about you? You've been a widow a long time. Have you been alone all those years, or have you thought about marrying again?"

She shrugged. "Once or twice."

"But?" His glance was keen, and this time it stayed pinned on her face.

"But it didn't work out. It was just one of those things. When I moved up here we drifted apart. Nothing earthshaking. No heartbreak or anything. Just an ending and a little . . . sadness."

He nodded as if he understood. "What about you?" she asked. "You said you were divorced what, nine years ago?"

"That's right. Lorraine was the Corville's only child, and we grew up together. I think we married more to please our parents than to please ourselves. When we both realized how bored we were with each other, we parted with no hard feelings on either side." Well, few hard feelings, he amended silently. Lorraine was one of those who had thought him heartless and ungrateful for failing to live up to their fathers'—and her own—expectations.

"You said that seven years was a long time to be

widowed. Nine years is even longer to be alone. Have you been?"

He looked somewhat taken aback at the bluntness of her question, but then he smiled. "Okay, I guess I deserve that. I pried and you answered. Like you, I haven't been alone the whole time, but there's never been anyone special. I don't see myself ever getting married again. I'm forty now. I think maybe I was meant to be a bachelor."

She shrugged. "I see." She didn't, but what could she say? She refilled their cups.

"You said 'once or twice,' " he reminded her. "You only told me about the once. What about the twice, Jillian?" He knew he had no right to probe, but, dammit, he wanted to know.

Again she shrugged. "It was about two years after Lance died. Maybe it was too soon. The breakup was my doing not his. But it still hurt."

He took her hand and curled his fingers around it. "More than just a drifting apart then? More than just a little sadness."

"More than that," she admitted, captured by the intense blue of his gaze.

"But it's over." He wasn't asking. She hesitated. She could lie and say that it wasn't, use that as an excuse for not seeing him again. But they had shared that kiss last Saturday, and she had invited him in tonight, and he had to know that it was over, that she wasn't pining for another man.

"It's over," she said, her gaze all caught up in his, her voice a mere thread of sound.

All he said was, "Good," as he drew her into his arms and bent his head to hers.

She welcomed his kiss even though part of her was telling her to resist this temptation. But the feel of his mouth was like a benison, a balm. And as his hands began to move over her body, she made a soft, encouraging sound and ran her hands into the thickness of his hair.

It felt so good, their coming together. His mouth on hers was hard and hot, and as he dragged her across his lap, she could feel the hardness of his legs, the strength of the arms that held her, the gentleness of his hand as it moved to her breast. Nothing had ever felt quite as good, quite as right, and she wanted it to go on and on.

With a soft cry, she opened her mouth to him, drawing him into her willingly as he deepened the kiss. Her entire body reacted to his tongue's penetration; her lower belly quivering with spasms, her nipples peaking and straining and yearning for the solidity of his chest against them. As if sensing her need, he turned her and lay down with her. Her hands found their way to the back of his shirt, discovering hard, rippling muscles under the softness of the cloth, and she stroked the taut planes of his waist, her fingers curling in sensuous pleasure, which wanted to give as well as to take.

He tugged his shirt free of his pants, and she breathed his name. His mouth left hers and moved slowly down her throat and across the top of her chest. He lifted himself half-off her as he quickly undid the buttons on her blouse and pushed it down her arms. She kept her eyes shut, her fingers gently raking the skin of his back. She was dizzy with wanting him, hot and trembling and vitally aware of the hardness of his need as it pressed against her lower body.

This was happening so fast, too fast, her mind tried to tell her, but she hushed it, wrapping her arms around him as she dragged in a great gulp of Mark-scented air.

His mouth made soft sounds against the tops of her breasts, skirting the lacy edge of her bra, and she strained up toward him, needing more, but he lifted his head and whispered her name as he spread her hair over her bare shoulders. "Jillian. Beautiful mermaid. Look at me."

She opened dreamy eyes and met the deep blue of his gaze, her lips parted and moist. He kissed her with little darting movements before taking her lips in another powerful, searching assault that made her moan deep in her throat. She nearly cried out when he slid his hard body off hers, but he wasn't leaving, only making it easier to touch her. He lifted his head, watching her face as he undid her bra and slid the cups off her breasts to run a tantalizing circle around each already hard nipple with one fingertip. She had to close her eyes again to stop the look of enchantment on his face from sending her out into orbit.

"No," he whispered. "Look at me. Don't hide your pleasure from me."

"Mark . . . I don't . . . I've never felt like this be—" Her breath rasped in and out as, eyes wide, she met his ardent gaze. Then she gasped, her lips parting as his cool hand cupped one warm breast. He looked down then, watching his thumb rub across the bursting peak, seeing the pink flush rise up her body. Bending his head, he kissed her almost reverently as his other hand cupped and stroked and teased the other nipple.

"Please . . ." The single word hovered between them as their gaze met and clung, and then she said it again, "Please, Mark!" and sobbed with relief when his mouth closed over one aching nipple, wetting it, heating it, pulling at it. He moved to the other one, his hand sliding down over her body, across her belly, curving over the small rise of flesh and bone at the juncture of her thighs, and she sighed as she moved her legs apart to allow his hand to stroke more firmly.

"Jilly? Jilly, are you home, dear?"

Her mother's voice broke the two of them apart as if they were truly guilty teenagers. She snatched her blouse around her and gasped for breath as she sat up, gaping unbelievingly at the staircase down which the voice had floated.

Six

"I'm downstairs, Mom," she managed to say, while Mark stood up, turned his back, and tucked in his shirt.

"What in the world are you doing down there at this time of night?" Her mother's voice was coming closer.

"I . . . having coffee with a friend. Is everything okay?" While she talked, she did up her bra and her blouse and was sitting erect, if wide-eyed, when her mother came down the stairs in a pink quilted bathrobe, her graying hair tangled, her glasses perched crookedly on her nose.

"Why, Mark! How nice to see you again," she said, obviously surprised to find him sitting in the big chair at the end of the coffee table, a cup of coffee in one hand. She smoothed her hair down and turned to her daughter.

"No, nothing's wrong, dear. I just woke up and found the kitchen light on and you not in your bed." She yawned, patting her mouth with the back of one hand.

"I'll say good night, then, now that I know you're safe."

When she had gone, Jillian carefully stacked the used dishes on the tray, and Mark, very subdued, carried it upstairs for her. She went with him to the door, and they stood there once more under the glow of the yellow porch light, saying nothing, just looking at each other, each one wondering exactly how "safe" things were between them.

"I only meant for that to be one, brief kiss, Mermaid, just a taste to see if you were still as sweet as you were last Saturday. It was too soon for anything like that to happen, wasn't it?" He looked deep into her eyes. "But if your mother hadn't gotten up . . ." His voice was a low rumble. "Are you sorry she did?"

She couldn't speak. She only leaned forward and let her forehead rest against his chest. For just a few moments his arms came around her, his cheek lay on top of her head. They stood like that, both afraid to make another move, both too shaken by what was rushing through them to risk ruining it, to dare to give it a name, even in their own minds.

Then he gently set her back from him, lifted her face with one palm under her chin, and said, "I have to leave now. I'm going back to town."

"Right now? Tonight?"

"Yes." He stepped down the stairs on light feet and was nearly at his car when her voice came floating out of the night to him.

"Drive carefully."

He turned and smiled at her. In the glow of the yellow bulb, with her hair all loose around her head, she looked like an incandescent fairy.

He smiled. "I'll do that, Mermaid. Thanks."

She laughed softly. "I could always send a taxi to follow you," she offered, but he just blew her a kiss, and then he was gone.

She didn't see him again or even hear from him for the rest of the week.

By the time her last Saturday night show was over and she was ready to leave work, she knew that he hadn't come up for the weekend. He hadn't called, and her escort had been the friendly taxi driver on Friday. Even now, as she pulled out of the lot, the taxi was behind her like a faithful guardian angel. She was glad of his presence, though, and was careful not to lose him or change her route home. She liked having him there. It was a reminder of Mark—not that she really needed one.

When she pulled into her drive, and the taxi swept on by, she got out into the steady drizzle that had been falling since noon. If it didn't quit, Amber's picnic was going to have to be postponed yet another time. She sighed. It didn't seen that either she or her daughter were destined to get what they wanted out of life.

It was still raining on Tuesday when she went back to work, but by the time she came out again, the clouds had big, black, starry holes in them and silver edges all around. She watched for the taxi, saw its headlights, and the two of them drove home. When it pulled away and she was about to get out, she saw a car door open across the street and sat very still, watching Mark approach. She didn't try to get out of her car. She felt too weak.

He opened the door and crouched beside her. "Hi."

"Hi." Her voice was a thready little sound.

"Hungry?" His expression said he was starved— for her.

"Yes." A picture formed in her mind of them on the couch in the rumpus room. What if her mother hadn't called out but had just come down? What if her mother had stayed asleep? Mark had asked her that question, and she hadn't been able to reply. She still wasn't sure in her own mind if she would have let things go much farther. But given the way he was touching her and the way she had been responding, she didn't know for sure if she would have been able to stop even if she'd wanted to.

That thought made her even weaker. She didn't know if she dared to invite him in again, because she knew that this time, even if her mother did wake up, she would be extremely careful not to come downstairs, not to let them know she was awake. She had apologized the next day in case she'd "interrupted" something and had laughed at Jillian's blush, saying, "Good heavens, Jilly! You're a grown woman! Surely you don't think I'd disapprove?"

Mark was smiling at her. "How about going to that all-night restaurant?" he asked. "If scrambled eggs are your thing, I think they could oblige." He paused. "And if they can't, I can. We could be at my place in under half an hour."

And there, she knew, they would not be disturbed.

Slowly she got out of the car. "The restaurant, please."

The scrambled eggs came with bacon and home fries and sourdough toast, but very little of it got eaten. They were too involved with each other as they talked and talked.

The conversation ranged from her marriage, which had been happy if tragically brief, to his, which had been not quite as brief but in its own way equally tragic. They discussed Chris and his inability to adapt to living with his father full-time.

They touched on religion and politics and books and movies, discovering some very similar tastes. Some subjects could, if permitted, lead to heated arguments, and others, if followed, easily could have led to heated exchanges of a different nature. Those latter topics they skirted very carefully, especially the subject of what had occurred Thursday night of the previous week.

Jillian learned that Mark's hair had started to turn white when he was twenty-five and that, yes, it was a family characteristic. He hoped his son wouldn't inherit it. She hoped he would, because she found his salt-and-pepper hair so wildly attractive.

Finally Mark stood up and took Jillian's hand, dropping money on the table as he led her back to the quiet luxury of his car. Silently they drove back to her place, and just as silently he turned her into his arms and kissed her for a long, sweet time.

"You're becoming very important to me, Mermaid, and I can't see as much of you as I want to, not with me in the city and you up here. What are we going to do about it?"

"I don't know," she said. "I don't really think there's a lot we can do."

"Don't kid yourself, Jillian. There are many thing we can do. I think we're just going to have to be . . . creative."

After another kiss, which she thought was one of the most creative ever because it created such a wild and wonderful turmoil in her blood, he let her go, and they walked to the house.

On the porch, he drew her into his arms and held her, not kissing her, just looking down at her as if trying to memorize her features.

"I'll be back, Mermaid. Your hours may be playing hell with my work and sleep schedule, but believe me, I'll be back."

And he was. Wednesday night, Thursday night, Friday, and Saturday. They went to "their" restaurant each time and spent an hour or two together, talking, learning about each other. He told her about the "elves" who worked on Elfshop toys, the mentally handicapped who otherwise wouldn't have a means to make a living, a way of showing themselves and the world that they were productive citizens. He told her of his deep pride in them and his hope that in time he would be able to expand the shop and branch out all over the country.

When he drove her back home, each night they spent many more minutes sitting in the car in the driveway, acting like teenagers until they ached so badly with need that they were gasping for breath and beaded with sweat.

On Saturday night, he said, "Let me come in, Jillian."

"I can't. You know I can't." She pulled herself out of his arms and wrapped her own around herself the way she did, he now knew, when she was tired or upset or frightened.

"I want you." His voice was hoarse. "If you won't let me come in, will you come home with me?"

"Mark . . . I—" She bit her lip, and he leaned over and kissed her.

"Don't do that. If anyone gets to nibble at your lips, it's me. Jillian . . . we can't go on like this."

"I know."

"Tomorrow," he said. "I want to spend tomorrow with you. All day. And all night."

"Mark . . ." It was hard to speak and hard to refuse him, because she was denying herself something she knew she wanted more than she had ever wanted anything before. "I can't. Sunday is my day with Amber. The only full day I ever have with her. It's important, Mark. I promised her a picnic. It's been put off for three weeks now, once because she was sick, once because I was too tired, and once because it rained. I can't do it to her again. I—" Her voice cracked. She cleared her throat and would have tried again, but he put a gentle finger over her lips.

"It's okay," he said. "I understand. Go on in, sweetheart. You're too tired for this now." For another moment he looked at her as if trying to read something in her face, then opened the door and got out to walk her as far as her door. There, just inside the living room, he turned her and kissed her hard again before breaking away from her and giving her a slight push.

"Good night, Mermaid," he whispered.

As she stood by her open window, she heard his car door slam and then heard him drive off. Loneliness descended upon her soul, and she quickly peeled off her clothes, got ready for bed, and slid gratefully between the sheets. She pulled the covers up around her shoulders, closed her eyes, and let sleep come over her in a huge, dark wave, not waking until she felt Amber's soft touch on her face.

"You were having a happy dream, weren't you, Mom? You were smiling while you slept."

Jillian gathered her daughter close and pulled her under the covers with her. "A very happy dream, my darling."

"What was it about, Mom? A handsome prince?"

"Nope," she lied. "It was about a lucky mom and her beautiful daughter who are going to have the best picnic ever today."

"I know!" Amber's face glowed. "Oh, Mom, it's going to be so much fun! I wanted to wake you up ages ago, but instead we just sat around talking about all the fun we're going to have, and where we'll go, and what we'll do, and that's almost as much fun as doing it will be. We've made all sorts of plans and there's enough food for ten people."

Jillian felt bad. Her mother hated picnics, and she'd had no idea she planned to go with them. Besides, Jillian was the one who had promised Amber this treat, so it seemed unfair that her mother should be the one to have spent the morning preparing for it. Her mother deserved a day off. She deserved far more than just one day off a week, in fact. As she had said to Mark, her mother deserved a life of her own.

Amber allowed her no more time for thinking of such things. She initiated a tickling match which culminated in the two of them tumbling off the bed rolled in the fluffy comforter. Amber escaped with a great deal more agility than her mother.

"Come on, Mom, get up," she said impatiently, tugging at the corner of the quilt, hindering Jillian in her attempts to extricate herself. "You get showered and dressed, and I'll go make sure Mark has enough coffee. He said he needed lots this morning because he didn't get much sleep last night. Hurry!"

"Amber!"

Jillian made a dive after her daughter and missed just as she swung open the door. Still half-wrapped in the comforter on the floor, she sat there staring up at the tall man in the doorway. Suddenly she became vitally aware that the pale aqua nightgown she wore barely covered her to the tops of her thighs and was nothing but sheer lace across the upper curves of her breasts and that it was held up only by tiny straps, one of which had slipped down and was in danger of allowing that side of the top to fall right off.

She felt the heat of his eyes on her, and her heart began to hammer in the way only he could make it do. She knew that he could see her nipples jutting out like hard little berries and that only made them pucker more tightly. A wild, pounding sensation began between her thighs and dizziness assailed her.

Pulling the comforter all the way over her legs and high under her chin, she swallowed hard and moistened her dry lips with the tip of her tongue. "What is going on?" she whispered, her eyes fixed on his face. "What are you doing here?"

As if sensing that her mother might be going to send her new playmate away, Amber ran to him and took his hand, clinging to it tightly, holding her breath as she waited for Jillian's verdict. Jilliar tore her gaze from her daughter's hope-filled fac< and looked again at the man.

A warm expression began in Mark's eyes, spread to crinkle their corners, then to bracket his firm mouth with deep creases as he smiled.

"What am I doing here?" he said. "Enjoying th< scenery. Do I dare to hope that those are you favorite picnic clothes, Mermaid? Or didn't yo remember there was a picnic planned for today' And," he said proudly, "I even packed the baske myself so you don't have a thing to do."

For another long moment she could only look a him, wondering if she were going mad, becaus< never had such joy flooded her spirits, never ha< she wanted to share a day with someone the wa' she wanted to share this day with the two peopl< who now stood hand in hand before her. Sud denly she laughed.

"I thought your medium was the barbecue. An< we like sandwiches for our picnics." She looke< stern and said, "Tell me the menu, and then I'l decide."

But they both knew she already had decided and that even if the menu was fried ice and clothes pins, she was going on that picnic.

"I'll get dressed," she said.

"I was afraid of that," he murmured softly.

He smiled when she returned in jeans and : skimpy T-shirt, her feet stuffed into grubby sneak ers, and her long hair tied back with a green scar that matched her shirt and her eyes.

"Chris!" she said, surprised to see Mark's son with him. "This is great! I didn't know you were here too."

He shrugged and scuffed one toe into the carpet. "Dad said I had to."

"Well, thank goodness for that," Jillian said, taking his hand and Amber's. "How could we have enjoyed our picnic if you weren't along?"

He allowed her to hold his hand for only a minute before he pulled away and marched for the door, head down. Mark followed him, saying, "Ladies, let's go. It's picnic time."

A canvas-topped Jeep was parked outside, and Jillian wondered just how many vehicles the man owned. She strapped Amber into the backseat beside Chris, placed Mark's picnic basket and the extra clothes and the blanket which she had thought to bring around their feet, then clambered up beside Mark. As he stopped at the end of her street, she put her hand on his wrist. "We have a special place we go that no one else seems to know about. Amber, would you mind if we took Chris and Mark there?"

"No, Mom, I don't mind. I'd like that!" Amber said with enthusiasm, grinning at Chris who looked at her as if she were some kind of interesting, harmless insect.

Mark smiled. "I'd like that, too, and thank you both for wanting to share a special place with new friends. Just point me in the right direction."

The picnic was a success. They ate lunch sit-

ting by a stream that babbled as Amber did. He
daughter's delight in their guests, and Mark's keen
humor as he bantered with her made Jillian smile
She only wished there was something she could
do to put Chris at ease. Luckily she hit upon
butterflies as a topic of conversation, discovering
he had an avid interest in collecting. But while he
willingly talked to her, he addressed his father
only when necessary.

The food was good and plentiful, and Jillian
pronounced the menu "just right," an approval
that made Mark beam as he handed her a crisp
green apple. Then, while Amber and Mark and
Chris splashed and waded in the cold water of the
creek, Jillian sat on the bank and watched their
antics. When Mark declared his feet were numb
he got out. Chris had left earlier to sit near Jillian
and Amber felt abandoned.

"Mom, come and wade," she said, and when her
mother refused, Amber looked sulky, then thought-
ful. Darting out of the cold water, she hunkered
on Jillian's other side, whispering in her ear, "Are
you 'barrassed because of Mark and Chris, Mom?"

Jillian hugged Amber's shoulders. "Maybe a little, hon."

"Mark wouldn't mind. He's nice. I like him.
Mom."

Jillian looked over at Mark, who had discovered
a laden huckleberry bush and was filling a plastic
tumbler with the delicious little red morsels—those
that made it past his mouth, she noticed. "I like

him, too, Amber. And maybe you're right, he wouldn't mind. But I would."

Mark saw her looking at him. "What are you two whispering about over there?" he called, his face alight with laughter. He knew perfectly well they were talking about him. Otherwise why would they have bothered to whisper?

"Girl talk," she answered, and sat back with her legs stretched out in front of her, feeling the heat of the sun on the top of her head, which was making her eyelids heavy.

Before she could fall asleep she got up, insisting they go for a walk.

"The bouncy tree, the bouncy tree," Amber said eagerly, and they set off across a patch of thick, damp moss that rose over their ankles. All four of them sat astride the low, bent branch of a cedar tree, bouncing hard on the springy limb.

Squished between Mark and Chris, Jillian felt as if her body was about to burst into flames. She couldn't move away from him unless she wanted to risk pushing Chris, who in turn might shove Amber right off the end of the branch. Perhaps Mark sat so close to her because he thought they were all in danger of falling off, but somehow, as his arms locked around her middle, holding her as closely as she held Chris, as Chris held Amber, she doubted it. For several moments, she gave into the temptation to lean her head back against his shoulder, but that encouraged him to place his lips at the corner of her mouth. It did such startling things to her insides, she had to lift her head. She wanted off the bouncy branch. She wanted out of Mark's embrace.

And she wanted what was happening to go on forever.

But finally even Amber's indefatigable legs gave out, and they were allowed to rest in the shade for several minutes before tackling a bluff that Chris wasn't at all certain they should try to climb.

"Jillian's got a sore leg," he said to his father in the surly tone he reserved for him. "She's been limping all day. Haven't you noticed?"

"It's okay, Chris," Jillian said, starting up the bluff with Amber right in front of her, telling him what she had told his father the one time he had asked if her leg was sore. It was what she told everyone who was kind enough to inquire if she'd hurt herself.

"It's a permanent limp, but it doesn't stop me from doing anything I want to do."

Oh no? she asked herself, glancing over her shoulder at Mark. *Doesn't it?*

He caught her glance and briefly wondered what it meant. He slowed down, holding back to watch the beautiful curve of her hips and thighs as she moved away from him up the bluff. She was as easy to watch on land as she was in the water, and he wondered if she had any idea just how he felt about her.

And, he asked himself, exactly how did he feel? He didn't know. All he knew was that when he wasn't with her, he wanted to be. He wanted to touch her all the time, to smell her skin, to feel her close to him, to hear the sound of her voice, of her laughter. He wanted to be able to take her into his arms and kiss her every time he saw her instead of having to share her with others—especially the men at the club. Again he recognized jealousy in himself and didn't like it. He was acting more like a man of twenty than one of forty.

Well, as he was a practical man of forty, he decided, he should be able to work things out logically and sensibly. All he had to do was put his mind to it. There was a solution to this dilemma he was in, and it was up to him to find it.

Jillian was sitting beside his son and her daughter when he came up behind her and crouched, looking down at the top of her golden head. The aromas of cedar and earth and moss clung to her skin and mingled with the fresh scent that was entirely her own. He put his hands on her shoulders, feeling the warmth of her skin through her blouse, lifting his face to the salty wind that blew strongly from the direction of the ocean, which they could see from the top of the bluff. But the only solution he could come up with to the problems that beset him was to take her in his arms and kiss the living daylights out of her. Only how could he, with two innocent children looking on? Damn, but she was getting to him!

"Look at that little boat go!" Amber said, standing up as a small aluminum boat bounced along, slapping across the wave tops. "Oh, I'd love to do that, Mom! Look at those ladies with their hair blowing back. I'd like to go that fast."

"But look at the men with their baseball caps turned around backwards," Mark said. "If they put them on the right way, the wind would blow them off."

"Then I wouldn't wear a hat at all," said Amber. "I like to feel the wind in my hair."

Presently the little boat slipped behind an island.

Back at the creek, they built a dam of rocks and sand to provide themselves with a small, still pool. In the pool they built islands of other rocks so that they could pretend their floating leaves were boats and that they were sailing from one island to another, always stopping to explore and discuss what their imaginations had conjured up.

Jillian was careful not to disclose too much of what her imagination kept coming up with, because she didn't think Amber and Chris would understand about a deserted island, a mermaid, and a handsome man—and Mark would understand only too well.

"Could we go on a real boat someday, Mom?"

"We did, hon. Remember, we went on that big ferry last year?"

"Um, yes, but I mean a boat that moves."

"Amber, that boat did move. It moved us from Keystone to Port Townsend and back."

Amber pushed her leaf carefully to the sandy shore of the creekbed and let it come to rest. "I mean like that little boat we just saw. Wouldn't it be fun to go in one that went real fast and made a noise like it did, slap, slap, slap? And have the wind in our hair?"

"Oh!" Now that she understood, Jillian smiled. Mark, too, smiled in sympathy.

"Sure," said Jillian. "One of these days we'll go in a boat that moves like that."

"Soon?" Amber asked.

"Soon," she said.

"Maybe even next Sunday?" Amber insisted.

"Sure," Jillian heard herself add rashly. She didn't have the faintest idea how she was going to make good her promise, but she would find a way. This time, she told herself, she wouldn't make Amber wait for the treat the way she had been forced to wait for the picnic. She would rent a boat if necessary. There was only one problem with that idea. If she did rent one, she wouldn't have the faintest idea of how to run it.

"I don't have a boat anymore, Amber," Mark said, "but I do have an open car you could ride in, and the wind would blow through your hair even better than it did in the Jeep today."

A picture flashed across his mind of Jillian in his open car with the wind in her hair. As if remembering, too, she reached up and pushed the green scarf higher around the base of her ponytail, her gaze locked with his.

He longed to snatch the scarf off her hair, let it flow free, feel it in his hands, on his face, on his chest, on his . . .

Oh, Lord! He had to control his thoughts. Amber and Chris might be blind to what was happening to him, but Jillian wasn't. He sensed that she was very much aware, however hard she might try to pretend otherwise. In her gaze he saw a flare of excitement that matched what was surging through him, before she lowered her eyes and hid behind her mascaraed lashes.

"I think I'd really rather go in a boat that bounces, thank you," Amber said politely.

Jillian sighed so softly that Mark barely heard her, and he reached out to take her hand in his. She refused to look at him again but squeezed his hand in acknowledgment of his offered comfort.

Amber must have heard the sad little sigh, too, because suddenly she hugged her mother around the neck, and Jillian hugged her back tightly.

Later, as a worn-out Amber took a nap on a blanket in the shade, Jillian sat quietly beside the stream, lifting handful after handful of sand, letting it slowly sift out between her fingers like time slipping away.

Seven

"What is it?" Mark asked quietly. "Ever since Amber asked to be taken out in a real boat that bounces, you've been blue. You shouldn't be, you know. She's a smart little kid. She knows she can't have everything she wants."

"Yes. But it's not just the things she wants that I can't give her, that I haven't been giving her. There are so many other things she needs."

Such as a father, she thought. The matter hadn't come up until Amber started kindergarten and saw that most kids had fathers, that even if they didn't always live in the same house as the mothers and children, they were around. They did things with their kids. And all Amber had was a mom and a grandma.

Oh, she had an aunt and an uncle who lived in

Oklahoma, and another uncle who was a long distance trucker, but she was lucky to see them three times a year. Seeing her respond to Mark really had brought home the fact that single parent families weren't what nature had intended for children.

Mark slipped his arms around her from behind, and she let her head fall back onto his shoulder. It felt so good to be held. He turned her face to his and brushed his lips lightly over hers, making her heart pound heavily inside her chest. He looked deeply into her eyes, so deeply that she felt a moment's fear and closed them, as if hiding her soul from him—hiding her building desire. She would have to control it soon, but at the moment she had no strength to lift her head from his shoulder, to move the hand that was stroking her face and neck.

"There are many things I need, too, Jillian," he said softly. "And first among them is you."

Her eyes popped open. He didn't hesitate when there was something he wanted, did he? Even when there were two kids within sight.

"Mark. This isn't a good time—"

"Is there ever going to be a good time, Jillian?" His gaze was so intense that she couldn't look away, and she didn't have an answer for him.

She could only say helplessly, quietly, "Don't. Please don't. Chris—"

"Chris is quite happily attacking that huckleberry bush on the other side of the creek. He isn't even in sight. And Amber is sound asleep. Besides, I only want to hold you and talk to you. Jillian, we have to make some kind of plans."

"But—" Her words were cut off by a kiss she was unable to move away from, and then Mark lifted his head, looking down at her with an emotion in his eyes that had never been there before.

"Oh, Lord, Jillian, ever since I first saw you, I've wanted you."

She tried to speak, but he covered her lips again with a swift and potent kiss, his hands turning her hair free to spill over her shoulder and his arm as he reached up, tangling his fingers in it. As his lips moved over hers, Jillian shuddered, but she was too aware of the difficulties giving in to him presented to be able to respond the way he wanted her to, the way she wanted to.

She remembered the feel of his hands and his mouth on her body, remembered how close she had come to forgetting. So many other times his kisses had beguiled her to the point of thinking nothing mattered but making love with him, yet each time she had managed to regain control of herself and the situation. She knew she wasn't being fair to him, but whenever she told him it had to stop, that they couldn't keep on like they were, he only agreed and told her that he knew it. But he meant that things were going to have to go farther, when what she meant was that they had to stop entirely.

Yet she didn't think she had the strength to

stop entirely. Not to see Mark, not to touch him, to have his kisses, to feel his arms around her, to hear his heart pounding inside his chest was something she couldn't bear to consider seriously. He was coming very close to melting her every defense, but deep inside she remained afraid that she still wasn't ready.

She pulled her mouth free, but continued to touch his face with her hands, softly, gently, as if she couldn't bear to lose contact with his skin.

"Mark! You just said it. Ever since we met you've wanted me. But what you met wasn't real. It was a fantasy. It isn't me you want, it's that mermaid you caught." Part of her wanted it to be true and another part rejoiced when he denied it vehemently.

"That's ridiculous! We both know I don't believe in mermaids." For a moment he thought guiltily of the brief time when he had done exactly that, only now it didn't seem possible that for even a second he could have permitted his mind to play that kind of game with him. Jillian Lockstead was all woman, and she was the woman he wanted.

"You have to know it's more than that."

He moved his hands over her body, shielding what he was doing from the children should either of them look in their direction. Jillian trembled and let herself sink into his warmth. His voice dropped to a low, seductive whisper as he continued. "Jillian, I want you so badly! From the moment you came ashore to me like some exotic creature out of a dream, I've wanted you. Every time I watch you perform it's torture. I can't bear the thought of any other man seeing you like that, wanting you, fantasizing about you. I want to have you exclusively. And I want to give you everything you've never had, everything you've ever wanted, both for yourself and for Amber. I want you to be able to stop worrying about your mother. I want—" He broke off, curling one leg around her hips, her legs bent so that she sat in the V formed by his. His hands were tight on her shoulders as he gazed into her face. He shook his head as if he didn't know what else to say to persuade her.

Then he added simply but with an urgency so compelling, she could barely resist it, "Jillian, say yes."

His hands molded her body, drawing her up against him as he knelt and pulled her with him, pressing their lower bodies together, showing her his heat and his desire and his need.

"Yes to what?" she asked, fighting against the danger of becoming totally lost in the sensuality of his touch. "I don't know what you want of me," she said, struggling out of his embrace. And it was only half a lie. She knew, certainly, that he wanted to make love with her. And Lord knew she desperately, achingly wanted the same, but she was so afraid, and there had to be more than that between them. Much more. She wouldn't settle for less, ever. Especially not under the circumstances. He'd have to know and want her anyway. He'd have to . . . love her.

"I'm not the fantasy creature you seem to think I am, Mark. I'm a flesh and blood woman, with needs and wants that you're stirring up like crazy, but I also have problems and worries and a mother and child dependent on me. I just can't turn my back on them. I don't want to."

"And I don't want you to either. I want you to share your problems and worries with me. I want you to come and live with me. You and Amber and your mother, too, if she wants," he added, his arms coming around her tightly once more.

"What?" This time she managed to break free completely. "You've out of your mind!" Ever conscious of her sleeping child, of Chris only fifty yards away on the other side of the creek, she kept her voice low but emphatic. "That's the craziest notion I've ever heard."

"It's not crazy, dammit. I'm being practical here, Jillian. I have it all worked out. I can help you with Amber. You've told me that there are things she needs that you feel you aren't providing. I have money. More money than I could ever begin to spend. To start with, I'll buy a speedboat and take her for a ride. And you say your mother's not well. I could hire the best doctors in the world, if that what she needs. I could—"

"That's not what she needs! She's getting what she needs—they both are—financially as well as medically!" Jillian said angrily, almost in tears.

How awful! She didn't want anything from him. If he had asked her exactly what she did want, she wouldn't have been able to tell him, but she knew it wasn't this . . . this "practical" solution to what he saw as her problems. He didn't have the faintest idea of what her problems might be, what worried her almost to the point of obsession, what kept her from having a good, honest relationship with any man, even one she was beginning to— No. She tried to break the thought off before it could form fully.

But the thought was there. The knowledge was there. The truth was there. She loved him. But it wasn't love he was asking her for, it wasn't love he was offering her. It was a practical solution to their need to be together in bed, and she suddenly was furious—with him, with herself, with fate for putting her in such a position. "What makes you think I would even consider moving in with a man I've known for three weeks?" she demanded in a hot, hissing whisper, her eyes snapping with anger.

"It took me less than a quarter of that time to know that I want you in my life, Jillian."

"In what part of your life?" Her voice cracked. "Am I to be part of your weekend retreat? You'll come to the club on Friday and Saturday nights and ogle me with the rest of the customers, take me out for an early breakfast and . . . and then what? Back to your place for a little sexual exercise? Or will we giggle and pretend we're teenagers in the basement at my place and hope my mother doesn't wake up? Does that turn you on, Mark? Acting like a sixteen-year-old again?"

She knew it was a terrible thing to say, but something compelled her to do it, and even when she saw the hurt in his face, she couldn't retract her words. She was shaking with fear and fury and pain. She sank down onto the sand again and half-turned from him, unable to go on looking at the agony in his eyes.

His voice was a low growl close to her ear as he said, "I want you out of that club, dammit. I want you with me all the time."

"How could I be with you all the time? Aren't you forgetting that you live in the city and I live here? I work here. I have a good job that I don't want to leave. And my mother lives here. I can't leave her on her own, and I doubt very much that she'd want to move. And what about Chris? How do you think he'd feel if I moved in with you only a few months after his mother's death?"

"Dammit, Chris knows and so do you that his mother and I were apart for nine years. It isn't as though her death released me to ask you to live with me. Chris likes you. You like him. We could be a family, Jillian. Think about it. The four of us together. Five, if you include your mom.

"But if you're right, and she wouldn't want to move, then I could hire a companion for her, someone she likes, someone you trust so you wouldn't have to worry about her. You told me that you only came back home because you'd gotten sick and then, after you were better, stayed for her sake. If she hadn't needed you, would you have stayed?"

Before she could reply, he had grabbed her and turned her, staring into her face again, his eyes blazing as he tried to convince her. He didn't know why it was so important, but suddenly getting Jillian to agree to live with him, getting her out of that nightclub had become the most important task in his life. He'd do anything to persuade her. "Or she could just live near us. I could buy her her own—"

"Mark, dammit, you sound as if you're trying to buy *me!*" she cried, crouching away from him, her eyes shimmering, the hair he had untied blowing around her flushed face and sticking in the wet streaks that trickled down her cheeks.

"Do you think you're the first one to come up with that idea? Though I must admit you're the most inventive so far. Your offer is a lot more detailed than any of the notes that have been sent to my dressing room, offers of money for my services as if I've put myself on sale simply by performing in a club. Well, let me tell you, Mark Forsythe, Jillian Lockstead is not for sale!"

He reached for her again, his hands clamping on her shoulders.

"Stop it!" she yelled, startling Amber who sat up and blinked sleepily, rubbing her eyes.

"Mom? What's wrong?"

Jillian moved quickly away from Mark and drew

in a deep, tremulous breath as he finally got to his feet and paced away from her, his head bent, his shoulders slumped.

"Nothing, honey," she said. "Just a . . . a hornet trying to sting me. Come on. It's time to get up now. The picnic's over."

Mark turned and looked at her for a long moment before he said quietly, "The picnic, maybe but not this discussion, Mermaid. Not by a long shot."

The solution to the problem of Amber's promised boat ride presented itself on Tuesday evening when Jillian got to work and found both Robin and Jim waiting for her with another offer from the congressional candidate. It wasn't the extra money that persuaded her to take the job, but the fact that when she demanded a small bonus in the form of a trip in the Zodiac for Amber, all three men agreed willingly.

The excursion was set up for the following Sunday, and Amber was an effervescent bubble of impatience for the rest of the week. It was all but impossible to keep her contained until then. But the day finally came, and Jillian sat in the rigid inflatable boat wishing for binoculars or at least her contact lenses so she could scan the shore and maybe get a glimpse of Mark. But her lenses were aboard the cruiser with her clothes, and she hadn't thought to ask for binoculars.

On the blur that was the shore she couldn't even begin to guess which direction, toward which barnacle-covered rocks she had been drawn and then been dashed against. She wondered if Mark was there watching and if he knew that she and Amber were in the boat.

As the small craft sped over the water, she was ready once more to go over the side with Robin, who was all suited up with scuba equipment as they neared the large, white cruiser where Ken Bristol waited along with his camera crew. This time, she had been promised, there would be no mistakes. Ken Bristol was going to use a very distinctive lure, one that she and Robin couldn't miss.

Again, her eyes swept the blurry shore as she wondered exactly where it was she had ended up last time. Was that a man standing on the rocks, or was it a tree? She wished she could see, but it was impossible.

She sighed. She wished she could stop thinking about Mark Forsythe, but that was impossible too.

She hadn't heard from him all week, so if he intended to continue the discussion she had terminated so abruptly, she had no idea when he meant to do it. Not that discussing it further would make a difference, but she would like a chance to apologize for having accused him of making a purchase-offer. Even as she had said the words to him, she'd known that she was wrong.

He'd panicked her, and she'd struck out at him the only way she knew how. She had to protect herself against the powerful pull he exerted on her—not just sexually, but on levels that went much deeper. His personality appealed to her too much. He was too easy to talk to. He answered a need she had long recognized within herself for a soul mate, someone she could lean on and who would be comfortable leaning on her.

She thought that it might be possible for her, with his help, to overcome the sickening fear she felt each time she thought of— She shuddered, remembering his kisses, remembering the tenderness with which his very presence surrounded her. Surely with him it would be all right, only . . .

She wanted a husband.

And Mark Forsythe had stated categorically that he did not want a wife ever again. All he had asked of her was to come and live with him. She—who had a child and a mother whose respect she cherished, to say nothing of a sister and a brother and several nieces and nephews—could never do that, not even for a caring man like him, and certainly not under the circumstances.

He cared deeply about his son; she had seen the gentle compassion with which he dealt with her own daughter. What he was doing for his "elves" was nothing short of saintly. And in the past weeks she had seen ample evidence of his concern for her. Even though they had fought, even though she had said cruel, hateful things to him and hurt him, she still was being shepherded home each night by her faithful taxi driver.

She missed Mark more each day. It wasn't something she could control. She thought about him all the time, jumped whenever the telephone rang. But it was never Mark, nor had he come to the club as far as she knew.

Now, as she watched Amber sitting perched on the back of the front seat of the Zodiac beside the man at the helm, her face held up to the wind, her small hands clutching tightly to the sides of the seat-back, Jillian reminded herself how important even this little jaunt was.

Amber was having a wonderful time, turning her head to let the wind whip her hair in different directions, opening her mouth wide to catch the salty drops that flew toward her, and holding up a hand to the wind and the spray, clearly enjoying the experience.

Jillian hitched herself to where her daughter sat. "Pretty good, huh?" she asked, as Amber turned a laughing face toward her.

"The best, Mom!" she shouted over the noise of the engines at the stern. "The absolute best!"

For Jillian the whole day became worth it.

Mark stood as he had three weeks before, fishing rod in hand, and tried to bring himself to cast the line out into the rippling water.

He could not. Each time he tried he remembered the very thing he was trying hard to forget, the sight of Jillian swimming toward him with that hook embedded in her breast.

That picture and so many more had lived with him this past long week while he had tried to get her out of his mind. It was impossible, and now he knew it. Something had drawn him back with a pull too powerful to resist, and he had been at the club the last two nights, watching her, aching for her, wishing he knew what was happening to him and why he couldn't get a grip on himself.

It was agony, being so near her and not being able to touch her, but it was ecstasy just watching her perform.

Her beauty enthralled him. He ached to hold her again, to feel her lips under his, to taste the sweetness of her mouth. He yearned to slowly peel away the barriers of her clothing—especially the mermaid suit—and see again the beauty he knew they concealed, to feel once more her hard, hot nipples jutting against his tongue. But sitting there and hearing the comments of the men around him made him grit his teeth and clench his fists in order not to break a few heads.

That described his relationship to date with Jillian Lockstead. From the very beginning, most of his feelings about her had caused him either agony or ecstasy.

There was the jealousy; all those evil-minded men and their foul talk. Couldn't they see there was a real, live, sensitive woman inside that suit, one who would hate the things they said about her, the things they discussed doing to her and then laughed about?

Also there was the fear. In spite of what she'd said about keeping her car in good repair, he couldn't help worrying. What if it did break down? There were too many dark streets she was forced to travel en route. There was even one undeveloped area she had to pass through. If she had trouble there, she'd be forced to walk blocks to the nearest telephone, and the thought of her doing that made him crazy inside.

No woman should be forced to travel home from work under those circumstances. And no woman of his would ever have to. No woman of his would have to work in a damned nightclub! If she were his wife, it wouldn't happen!

He sat down abruptly on the hard rock. His rod and reel threatened to slide into the sea, and he caught the butt end of the rod, setting it into a safer location, wondering where that extraordinary idea had come from.

Since his divorce he had not once contemplated marrying again. And it wasn't as though he was really giving it serious thought now, he told himself. It was just that damned jealousy and the fear he felt for her safety. He wanted her, true. He had asked her impulsively, and much too soon in their relationship, he now acknowledged, to come and live with him. No wonder she had taken offense.

Practical or impractical, sane or insane, the

woman had done something to him. If it was the last thing he ever did, he vowed, he would get her out of that tank, get her off public display and into his bed until he had her completely out of his system, because, like it or not, he wanted her all to himself.

He saw the fast-moving Zodiac come sweeping around the tip of the point, heading in his direction, and he concentrated on it, glad of the distraction. A child with long, dark hair flying loose was seated high in the bow, another figure sat at the wheel, and one sat low in the middle of the boat. Seemingly oblivious of anyone else, the operator of the small craft sent it zipping along, throwing a huge wash that dashed up on the shore nearly to Mark's feet, sending other boats into frenzied rock and roll maneuvers.

Over the scream of its engines a high, childish voice shouted, "The best, Mom! The absolute best!" the sound carrying clearly ashore.

Mark recognized that voice and stood up quickly, shading his eyes.

The Zodiac came to a halt near the largest of the boats anchored in the bay. It was a thirty-foot raised-deck cruiser with shiny white paint and a flying bridge from which a man in a gold braided cap gave gestured instructions to the operator of the Zodiac.

All at once Mark recognized the cruiser too. The *Andrea!* The small boat disappeared around her stern and was out of sight for several minutes.

When it reappeared, only the man at the wheel and the child in the bow beside him were visible, and it didn't take the cameraman bracing himself in the stern or the other cameraman on the bridge to tell Mark what was going on.

But what he couldn't understand was *why* it was going on when he had heard Jillian adamantly refuse to do a retake of the scene. Then, suddenly, he understood.

This was Amber's bouncy boat ride.

Damn her! Didn't she see this as "selling herself" just as much as letting him do things for her and Amber would be? He sighed, the whiplash of anger that had snapped through him subsiding. No. Of course not. To Jillian it was a job, and presumably the candidate hadn't asked her to go to bed with him, or if he had, she'd have refused both his offer and the job. Presumably, the candidate wasn't the clumsy, idiotic fool that Mark Forsythe had been. Presumably—though he thought it was highly unlikely—the candidate wasn't on the verge of falling in love with a mermaid.

And he was. No, he was more than just on the verge. He had done it.

The thought was stunning, and he had to sit down again while he absorbed it fully. Oh, Lord, yes, he loved her. That explained the jealousy. It explained the fear he felt for her safety. It also explained why it was so damned important for him to have her come and live with him.

But was that really all he wanted from her? All

she wanted from him? Oh, heavens, was that what had offended her so badly? Was it the way he had put it, the lack of commitment he seemed willing to give? Was that what she wanted from him? And was he, when it came right down to it, willing to give it?

For long moments, he closed his eyes against the glare off the water, thinking deeply, wondering if it would be possible, if it could be the answer. He had sworn he'd never do it again, that it was too much trouble, that marriage changed things too much, made people look at each other differently. But now he wasn't so sure.

He already had seen Jillian in so many different ways, looked at her in her many guises, and he had wanted her in every one of them.

He'd seen her first in her mermaid persona, a little bit of magic that took his breath away and filled his soul with joy. He remembered the look in her eyes after the first time they had kissed, and the compassion on her face while they discussed Chris. He had been touched by the tenderness she showed her daughter, by the fierce love shared by the pair of them, and he admired the concern she had for her mother.

He smiled, thinking of how she had looked the second time he'd followed her home. Dressed in jeans and a blue blouse and with her hair like a golden cloud tumbling around her shoulders she had tilted her chin up and said in that soft, musical voice of hers, "You followed me," as if she were amazed that anyone would care that much about her welfare. Of course. She was always so busy looking out for others, she probably never noticed that she needed looking after herself.

He had seen her that same night rosy and weak from his kisses, passionate and giving. He had wanted her with such raging desire in his blood that, when he'd left, he'd sworn never to return, because wanting of such magnitude was dangerous to a man like him who valued his freedom.

But it was that same desire that had driven him back to see her show and to follow her home again, to sit in that restaurant with her and talk until her eyes were so sleepy, she could barely keep them open. He'd been rocked by the swift surge of tenderness that had made him want to lift her up and carry her home, because when she was tired, her limp was worse.

He thought, too, about the way she had looked sitting on the floor of her bedroom all tangled up in the quilt that had covered her to just above her knees, and the sheer nightie she wore that covered very little of everything else. He had hated the thought of her getting dressed, yet when she'd come out of her room in a green T-shirt, it had been all he could do not to grab her. Later, of course, he had grabbed her, and he had said and done stupid, impulsive things, but he meant to make up for it if she would let him.

He would go to her house, ask politely for a date, take her somewhere quiet and private for dinner—maybe he could talk her into coming to his house—and then if it seemed just right, if he could keep himself under control, he would tell her he loved her and wanted to make slow, wonderful, beautiful love with her—all night long.

And then he would ask her to marry him.

Eight

Mark became aware that he was trembling as he sat there, that he was as scared inside as he'd been the first time the sergeant had hollered "Next!" and it was his turn to jump out of the airplane. But he had made the jump and survived. And he'd make this one.

Or he wouldn't survive.

The little boat was bouncing around like a cork, and even from a distance, Mark could see that Amber was no longer perched on the back of the seat but huddled down on it. Only her head and shoulders were visible behind the rounded side of the boat, but he could see one hand tightly gripping the rope that ran the length of the hull. Apparently now she didn't think her excursion was the "absolute best."

A tall, white-clad figure appeared on the stern of the cruiser as he had the previous week, fishing rod in hand, and expertly flipped his lure and sinker out over the side, then began feeding line down into the water. Both cameras focused on the man, but now and then one of them would pan the surface farther out or sweep slowly along the shoreline. Most of what was happening was happening on the far side of the cruiser, and it seemed to be taking a long time. Ten minutes then fifteen dragged by while Mark waited for a glimpse of his mermaid. From across the water came the sound of Amber's clear, childish voice once more. "Mr. Larson, how long will my mom have to stay down there?" She sounded tearful.

He didn't hear the man's reply, but it didn't seem to satisfy the little girl, because she moved from the bow seat, awkwardly clinging to the side, toward the center of the boat. The man with the camera was paying her no more heed than the one behind the wheel, and as she stood, teetering, Mark's heart stopped. What in the hell was the matter with those men, letting a six-year-old child scramble around unaided in that damned little rubber raft?

He saw her hunker down, gripping the front of her life jacket. He saw that her head was drooping, but after a moment she lifted it. Whatever she said was too quiet for him to hear, and he leaped from rock to rock, racing out onto a long point exposed by the low tide in order to get closer to her.

"Mr. Larson, how much longer?" Mark heard her ask again.

"I don't know, kid. Look, you wanted to come. Nobody forced you. So if you're bored with waiting around, don't blame me."

"I'm not bored. I don't feel good."

Of course she didn't feel good, thought Mark. What the heck was the matter with Larson? Why didn't he start the engines in order to keep the bow pointed into the waves? That way, the rolling and pitching wouldn't be quite so uncomfortable.

He was about to shout out his suggestion when the two men in the rubber boat consulted in indecipherable voices. He heard the engines rumble to life, and he sighed with relief. They were going to put her aboard the big boat where she'd be much better off, he thought.

But to his amazement, the cameraman was the only one who left the Zodiac, leaping onto the rocks of a small island offshore, shouting to the men on the cruiser, "Gonna have to get my shots from here. It's too damn rough out there to focus right."

Then, quickly, he held up a hand. "There she is. Now, quiet, everybody."

Of course. That was why the engines were shut off, why the boat had been sent to drift out of the range of the cameras. Suddenly with a disgusted shout Ken Bristol, congressional candidate, flung his rod to the deck in a fit of temper that would have done credit to a four-year-old. "Oh, hell, the damned line broke."

Jillian must have surfaced then, because he went on, "For Chri . . . Pete's sake, Jillian! What the hell are you trying to do? You're going to have to go down again, and this time don't put up so much of a fight. We need to make it look good, but not so good that you break the line. Where the hell's that diver with her air supply? Hey, Robin . . . over here. Get her back down there, and this time make sure she doesn't break the line. Okay? Everybody ready?"

Obviously everybody was because another rod was put into the candidate's hands, and again the cameras panned the water, the fisherman, and the extremely photogenic shoreline, waiting for the moment when they would have in their viewfinders an even more photogenic mermaid who would bring much publicity to the candidate's "Clean Up the Oceans" campaign.

What they did not photograph, however, was a little girl leaning over the edge near the stern of the Zodiac being sick, and the look of utter disgust on the face of the man at the helm who only glanced at her over his shoulder and then turned away.

Mark muttered a curse, peeled off his shirt, and hit the water in a shallow dive. He stroked strongly toward the bouncing boat. As he reached the side, the man at the wheel never even noticed him, so intent was he on watching what was happening on the cruiser.

He noticed, though, when Mark reached up and pulled himself half-out of the water beside the sick little girl and said, "Amber, honey, it's Mark. Want to get off this boat?"

She opened her eyes and looked at him woefully. She was crying. She nodded and clutched at his wrist. She sniffed and tried very hard to smile.

"Mark, I got sick."

"Hey, Mac, get the hell outta here," shouted the man in charge of the rubber boat. He got out of his seat behind the wheel and started to make his way back to where Mark hung beside Amber. "There's something important going on here."

"This," said Mark, putting his hands under the arms of the child who hung over the side, her eyes shut, a look of utter misery on her face, "is a hell of a lot more important." With that, he drew her down into the water with him and kicked away from the boat.

"Hey! What the hell . . ." The man, Mark noticed, managed to keep his voice to a whisper in spite of what was happening. "You can't do that!"

But Mark already had.

"You come with me for a swim, baby doll," he said, swiftly stroking with one arm to take them farther away from the man who had now lifted an oar and was stretching it out toward them.

Amber showed no shock, no fear, only kept her wide, trusting green eyes pinned on Mark's face.

He kept on talking as he moved her away from the boat, out of reach of the oar the man now aimed threateningly like a javelin. Mark knew it was an empty threat. As empty as the whispered order that he "bring that kid back here, right now, or else!" The man was a true loyal functionary, one who couldn't think for himself, not even when he saw the child in his care being snatched from before his very eyes. He had been told to keep quiet, and keep quiet was all he could think to do.

As concerned as the man might be about his charge having been kidnapped, clearly he put a whole lot more importance on not raising his voice or starting his engines and disturbing the filming that was going on over on the far side of the boat.

"You can come to my house until your mom's finished work," Mark said to Amber, grabbing hold of the loop of cloth at the top of her life jacket and rolling over onto his back, towing her along with him. "Okay?"

She tilted her head back and gave him another smile, this one more assured. "Sure, Mark. And you can let me go. I can swim, you know. Even without a life jacket. You just stay beside me so I know which way to go." She was worried, but determined not to show it.

Mark nodded solemnly. This was one very little girl in a very big chunk of water, and he thought she was showing a lot of guts. With deliberately *un*whispered instructions to the man in the Zodiac as to where Amber could be collected, he swam away with the bobbing, life-jacketed child toward the shore, talking gently and reassuringly to her all the while until his feet bumped up against the rocks and he waded ashore, carrying her.

Mark decided it was almost as much fun as catching a mermaid. Especially knowing that just as soon as her job out there was finished and his mermaid found out what had happened, she would come swimming after her child.

He laughed aloud as he stood Amber on her feet and hauled the wet life jacket off her, leaving her in soaked shorts and a T-shirt. He led her to his house, wondering what in the world he was going to dress her in. He decided that Edward would be the one to take care of that. He was going to have to go back to the edge of the water and wait for Jillian. He found he was crazily, childishly, excited about his next meeting with Jillian Lockstead, Mermaid.

He was sitting on the rocks twenty minutes later, while Amber, who had captivated Edward completely, played with the vanful of furniture and the house he had brought with him to give to her this weekend in spite of her mother's protest. He had left the elderly man and the little girl arguing like a pair of opposite-minded interior decorators over the placement of furniture in the rooms of the log house.

He sat there for what seemed like much too

long a time, watching the Zodiac drift. Then it disappeared around the other side of the cruiser, and he started to feel flutters of anticipation inside his stomach, much the way he had when he had been thirteen and had decided that he was going to try to kiss Shelly Morton.

As he gaped in shock, the cruiser's engines started up with a deep rumble, the anchor was pulled back aboard, and the big boat left, Zodiac in tow. Mark stood, shouted Jillian's name, and even though he knew no one aboard the yacht could hear him, he shouted again. Then, as the large swell of its leaving came rushing ashore, Mark glanced down and caught a glimpse of blue-green just under the surface, a sheen of golden fire swirling in a coil. At that moment he was off the rocks, into the water, and gathering up his mermaid once more.

It was awkward this time because she wore scuba gear. He felt her arms, icy cold, come around his shoulders, and staggered back until he was sitting on a rock in water up to his middle. He peeled the mask off her as she spat out the mouthpiece.

"Where's Amber?" she demanded, and then sat forward so he could relieve her of the tanks and flotation vest.

"Having a wonderful time with Edward. It was a case of love at first sight. Another one."

Jillian stared at the tanks he had removed from

her back. They floated, bobbing, bouncing against the rocks, hoses looking like fat, orange snakes.

Another one? She looked up at him, her eyes wide.

And then Mark did what he had wanted to do the first time he had hauled his mermaid out of the depths. He placed his lips over her blue, salty ones and kissed them until they were warm and sweet and parted for him. Her arms were around him, and she was responding as wildly and as hotly as he'd known she could, dreamed she would. Even more than he'd remembered, more than he'd hoped, she was answering his most urgent question whether she knew it or not.

Her mermaid suit was rough against his arm, its scales pressed into his legs, and the thick-textured fabric over her breasts kept him from touching her as intimately as he wanted to. But this time there was no babbling little voice in his mind telling him that it was impossible for him to be holding a mermaid in his arms. When he lifted his head and stared at her beautiful face for what seemed half a lifetime, once more he felt a bubble of joyous disbelief welling up inside him. Because, even if in his arms he didn't truly hold a mermaid, in his heart he again held magic, and in his soul there was a brand new world.

And this time he knew it was for more than just one moment.

Slowly Jillian opened her eyes and said, "Oh, my," before she felt his mouth descend onto hers again, felt its incredible heat, felt once more the hardness of his chest and the breadth of his shoulders and knew she had been waiting for him all her life. She gasped, her lips parting to admit his tongue, and a delicious heat rose inside her, warming every part of her, even her chilled skin.

When he next lifted his head, they stared at each other for several seconds. "Oh, my, is right," he said, and she smiled weakly, feeling as if she had just tried to take a breath from an empty air tank. By the time she had managed to inhale, she was light-headed, dizzy, ready simply to let go and drift.

As their mouths crushed together once more, the wash from a passing boat caught her tail and lifted it, tilting them backward. Then they were both underwater again, arms and legs and tail tangled, her hair floating across his face. His hands caught the strands and shoved them aside as his lips reluctantly left hers and they surfaced.

It was all they could do to catch their breath before they were locked together again in a tight embrace, sitting waist-deep in the water, clinging to each other, oblivious to their surroundings.

"I wondered," she said moments later, running her fingers through the thick, dark brown mat of hair on his chest. "I wondered what it would be like."

"You knew what it would be like the same as I did," he said roughly, his apparent confidence a thin mask for his insecurity. "You spent all week wanting to kiss me again, just as I spent all week lying awake aching for you. Didn't you?"

She nodded, smiling happily at him. "Only I didn't remember exactly what the impact would be," she admitted.

"I didn't expect it to be quite that . . . uh . . . impactful either," he said in a ragged voice. "If just a kiss after a week of missing you is so explosive, what is it going to be like making love when the time comes, Mermaid? Think about that one."

Her gaze flew to his face. Her hands stilled on his chest.

Mermaid. He still thought of her as the fantasy creature he had caught on his line. And maybe it was just as well. She forced herself to smile and swam a few feet away from him. Catching onto the air tanks they had let go of earlier, she lifted them onto the shore, set her floating mask and snorkle beside them, out of reach of the waves, then flipped onto her back, stroking away from him, thinking about what he had told her—not that she needed his encouragement. She'd thought about little else since she'd last seen him.

Mark grinned and dove after her, lifting her high as he carried her carefully up over the barnacle-encrusted rocks until they were lying on the hot shale with the sun beating down on them. He closed his hands over hers, flattening them to his chest. She wanted to pull away, but her strength was puny compared to his, and her will was even more so as she lost herself in the blue of his eyes.

He swallowed hard, his eyes burning into hers as he tugged her hands up around his neck.

"Jillian. When?"

"When?" she echoed, her heart going wild.

"Yes, when," he said impatiently. "When can we be together?"

"We . . . we are together, Mark," she said. "I mean . . . we're in the same place."

"That's not what I mean. Not what I want. I want . . ."

Dammit, he hadn't meant to do it this way! He had planned it so differently, all slow and soft and sweet with candlelight and music. But his need for her overwhelmed him and he heard himself blurt out, "I'm in love with you, Jillian. I want to marry you. I want you. And I know you want me."

"No! No, you don't want to marry me!" She pushed him away. "You said you never wanted to get married again. And you don't know anything about me, Mark. You don't know—"

"I know I love you," he said. "Sure, until today I didn't think I wanted to get married again. But while I was waiting for you, watching what was going on out there, thinking of you down in the cold water where you didn't want to be, I wished there was some way I could have the right to demand that those men get you out of there. I realized that there was only one way for me to have that right, that marriage is the only thing that makes any sense for us."

"Mark, no, we—"

"We have to be together, Jillian. You know we do. Because not only do I love you, but you love me, don't you? Tell me," he said hoarsely. "Jilly, tell me you love me!"

It was true, but she didn't want to admit it. She never had felt more frightened. Reaching up, she pulled his head down and kissed him, curving her body to fit the hardness of his. She didn't want to think. She didn't want to talk. She simply wanted to feel the things that only he could make her feel. She wanted to be stirred as only he could stir her. She had adored her former husband Lance, but never once had his lovemaking done to her what even one of Mark's kisses could do.

He broke the kiss and lifted his head, gazing at her, enraptured. "I didn't think I'd ever think in terms of forever, Mermaid, but now I am."

"Oh, Mark . . ." She wanted to cry. Didn't he understand? This couldn't last. He was looking at a mermaid, for heaven's sake, and it was the fantasy he thought he loved. But when he knew the reality, when he saw the real Jillian, his love would come crashing down with a roar like the shotgun blast that had roared in her ears as it changed her life forever.

"Mark . . . Please. Stop it. We aren't going to be together. Not the way you mean. We aren't going to make love. This is something that will pass.

Okay, so we're both attracted to each other, but it isn't real. It's all part of the pretense of my act. That's what you have to understand. None of what you're feeling is real."

He snatched her close again, kissing her until her head spun. He dragged her hand down his body, placed it where it was most needed, and said in a raspy voice, "Oh yes it is! If that's not real, Jillian, then I don't know what is."

It was real. And so was her reaction, so were her feelings. She swallowed hard and forced herself away from him.

She started to say something, but he cut her off, wrapping his arms around her and carrying her higher up the rocks to sit in a little crevice out of the wind. He hauled her air tanks above the high tide mark, and then returned to her, folding her close in his arms.

"Listen to me," he said. "I want you to know how sorry I am, how I wish I'd kept my mouth shut instead of spouting off like I did last Sunday. I got carried away by my feelings. I said things I shouldn't have said. I said things it was too soon to say, and you got the wrong impression of me. Hell, it's still too soon, but I can't help myself anymore than I could then. But believe this, I wasn't trying to buy you, Jillian. I wasn't trying to act like one of those creeps who send notes to your dressing room. I was trying to get you out of that dressing room, out of that tank where they can all ogle you and make crude comments about you. All right, so I didn't know it at the time, but I wanted all that because I love you. If I'd known then, I'd have said so, and it wouldn't have sounded so bad, so cold and calculating.

"I spent all week telling myself to let you go, that this was all just a passing thing, but all that time, too, I wanted to phone you and was afraid to. I didn't want to hear you say you wouldn't talk to me. For the same warped reasons, I didn't follow you home the last two nights, but let the taxi driver do it. But I was there, Jilly. In the club. I sat there all Friday evening, all Saturday evening, through each of your shows and listened to the speculation, listened to the filthy fantasies those men were spouting, and I wanted to kill. I want you out of there. I want you safe. I just . . . want you. But I'm not like them, love. I don't want to buy you. I just want to marry you."

"Oh, Mark, I know that." Tears flooded her eyes, and he kissed them away. "I'm sorry too," she said finally, when she could speak. "I said awful things to you, accused you of things I know you didn't mean. Mark, forgive me."

"I'll forgive you anything, if you'll just say you love me and will marry me!"

She looked at him and hoped he could see the love in her eyes, because she couldn't say the words. Nor could she tell him that to be married to him was the thing she wanted most in the world. She could feel the tension in him as he waited for her response, feel the hurt in him when it didn't come, but then he smiled and touched her face with the broad tip of one thumb, drawing a line from her brow to her chin.

"Okay," he said, "I can wait." He scooped her up and carried her toward the house, hearing the clang of the gate as it shut behind them, locking them in. Together. He smiled in satisfaction. He had brought his mermaid home, and this time he wasn't going to toss her back. This time she really was a keeper.

Nine

He took her back to the patio and sat her on a chair near the pool, crouching beside her, stroking her damp hair back with a tenderness that made her ache inside.

"How about we get you out of that suit?"

Suddenly she went white, then her cheeks flared with color. Mark remembered the last time he had suggested she remove her costume and her sharp, almost panicked refusal. He frowned and cradled her cheek on one hand. "What's wrong, Jillian?"

"Nothing. Nothing at all," she said, but he was sure she was lying and was about to call her on it when she laughed, seeing Amber come out of the house wearing a huge gray sweatshirt with the sleeves rolled up and a blue silk tie tied around the middle. Her feet were bare, and her legs stuck out from beneath the big shirt like little sticks.

"Hey, Amber! Nice dress," she commented, reaching out to hug her daughter. "You feeling okay now, love? Mr. Larson told me you got sick and that Mark came to get you. Why didn't you tell me you didn't feel well? I thought you were having a great time."

"I was, Mom, honest. It was lots of fun when we went fast and bounced and there was wind in my hair the way it was with those ladies. It was just when the little boat rocked and rocked and rocked and nothing made it sit still that I got sick. I sure was glad to see Mark, Mom."

"I bet you were, hon. Did you tell him thanks?"

"Yes, and Mr. Carson gave me peppermint tea to make my tummy feel better, and Mark gave me a present. Want to see?"

"Sure, but you'll have to bring it to me. I don't want to go inside in my suit."

"Why don't you take it off, then you can come and play with me and Mr. Carson. He found me some things to wear, and I bet he could get you something too. Come on, Mom, I want you to—" Amber broke off. "Oh," she added softly. "I forgot."

Then, turning, she tore away, calling over her shoulder, "I'll get Mr. Carson to help me bring it all out." She was back before Mark could think of a way to phrase the question that was running through his mind. What was it about Jillian and that mermaid suit that Amber had "forgot" and that made Jillian pale at the very thought of removing it?

Amber returned with her arms full carrying a moving van, followed by Edward with the big log house.

"Mark!" Jillian didn't know whether to laugh or cry or get mad. "I said I'd get her one for Christmas. You didn't have to do this." She slithered off the chair onto the pool deck and watched as Amber carefully placed sofas and chairs and beds and tables and refrigerators in appropriate places. Then, when she'd had it all neatly arranged, she carefully dismantled each room and loaded the furniture into the van.

"Where's Chris?" Jillian asked, hoping he wasn't in his room brooding while the rest of them were out here having fun.

"He's spending the weekend sailing with friends of mine," Mark explained. "They have a son his age who's celebrating a birthday this weekend."

Suddenly Amber leaped to her feet and said, "Mom! What time is it?"

"Oh, my gosh! Billy's birthday party! Amber, I forgot! Mark . . . ?"

"It's half-past twelve," he said.

"It's okay, hon. You can make it. If Mark would be good enough to drive us home, we'll have plenty of time. Billy lives next door," she added for Mark's benefit.

"Why not let Edward take her?" Mark asked quickly as the elderly man came out pushing a cart filled with sandwiches, a salad, and glasses of iced tea. "You'd do that, wouldn't you, Edward? Take Amber home in time to get to a birthday party?" He gave the man Jillian's address. "Didn't you plan to go to your daughter's place for dinner this evening? You could go early and spend the whole afternoon with her."

Edward smiled blandly as he looked from Mark to Jillian and back again. "Yes, sir. I could do that, and I'd be happy to take Amber home on my way." Edward narrowed his eyes on Mark and added, "One condition, though?"

Mark grinned. "All right, all right. Take the Mercedes."

"Now, wait a minute," said Jillian, feeling that this entire thing was being arranged without her having any kind of a say in the matter. "I need to get home, too, you know. I want to get . . . changed."

"If you want to get changed, I have plenty more bathrobes, any of which are yours to keep," said Mark, lifting her back onto her chair and handing her a plate of salad. "We can't waste all this food. Okay?"

"Okay, Mom? Please? I don't want to be late for Billy's party." Amber was bouncing up and down, holding Edward Carson's hand.

Jillian looked from Amber to Edward to Mark and caved in like a popped balloon. "Okay," she whispered, feeling sick with apprehension as she saw her daughter walk off hand in hand with her new friend, leaving Jillian and Mark completely alone together for the very first time.

She wondered if Edward even had a daughter with whom he had planned to spend the evening, or if the whole thing had been neatly arranged in a manner long since perfected by him and his boss.

"You see?" Mark said when the Mercedes had been gone for fifteen minutes and he had eaten his salad, Amber's, and half of Jillian's. "You see how well Amber and I get along? How much she likes Edward? I like her, and I like your mother, and remember how well you got along with Chris? He likes you, Jillian.

"We could do it, sweetheart. Be a family. All of us together, loving, learning, growing, being complete together."

She shook her head then slid from her chair to the deck and into the pool, where she felt more sure of herself. In the water she truly was complete as she swam expertly toward the bottom, curved her tail and surfaced, pushing her hair back from her brow, looking at him as if she didn't quite know where they were going to go from there. She looked like a cross between a frightened girl and a seductive temptress, and he thought that maybe even she wasn't sure just which she was at the moment.

There was still a faint, pink scar where her cut had healed. Even from where he stood Mark could see it, and it reminded him of the day he had caught her. That day he had hated the thought of having to let her go because she was a novelty. Now he knew he would never be able to let her go, because she was his life.

But something was wrong, and if she wouldn't let him in on it, there was no way he could make it better.

"Jillian," he said, "come out. Please, love. We have to talk."

Again she bent and dove to the bottom, sweeping from one end of the pool to the other before coming up for breath in the center.

"Come in with me, Mark. Come and fulfill every man's fantasy. Swim with the mermaid."

He stripped off his shorts and dove in naked, letting her catch his hand and draw him under the surface. Opening his eyes, he saw her hair swirling around her face, saw her beautiful mermaid body curling and twisting as she slid around him, arousing him as her mouth came to his and she kissed him deeply, silently speaking of the love she felt for him, the need, the desire. Her arms clung to him, her fingers stroking his back, his naked buttocks, and he hated the suit she wore as he had never hated anything else before, because somehow he sensed that it had something to do with her reluctance to believe in his love, to accept it, and to become part of his life.

When his feet touched bottom, he kicked hard and shot to the surface, still holding her, their mouths still locked together. As the air hit their faces, they broke apart, gasping.

Catching her hands in his he said, "I don't want you to be a mermaid, Jillian, whatever you think, that's not what I want of you. I don't want a fantasy. I want the real thing. I want it all."

She looked at him silently for a long time, and then he realized the beads of water running down her cheeks weren't coming from her wet hair but from her eyes.

He swam with her to the shallow end, where they had sat once before.

"What is it, my darling?" he said, wiping her face with the palms of his hands. "Jillian, let me in. Let me help. Oh, sweetheart, I want so badly to fix it!"

"You can't fix it, Mark. Nobody can. And you can't love me, either, because I only have one leg."

"*What?*" Mark's look of shocked horror undid her completely, and she wrenched herself away from him, diving underwater, swimming fast and furiously, her massive tail pumping as it pushed her in long, sweeping glides that he was incapable of keeping up with. He chased her until he was exhausted and had to cling to the side of the pool.

Finally, getting out, walking unsteadily up the steps, he stood leaning on the back of a chair, gasping for breath. "All right, Jillian. So you can outswim me the way a porpoise can outswim a slug. But you can't make a statement like that and then run away from the consequences. You—"

She dove under the water again, back to where she didn't have to hear him, back to where she didn't have to see him, back to where she could try to forget the look on his face when she told him the truth about herself. She didn't know why he wanted to talk about it. Couldn't he see that there was nothing to say?

She surfaced at the center, well out of his reach, and saw him standing there waiting. As soon as her head was out, he went on as if she hadn't interrupted him by diving. "You have to come out of there sooner or later, because if you don't, I'm going to drain the pool."

She dove again. He wouldn't do that. She knew he wouldn't do that to her, leave her high and dry and stranded in the bottom of an empty pool. At least she understood that much about him; he understood that she needed the cloak of her costume and the water. She wanted to be able to shed both, but it was simply too hard. Why didn't she have enough courage? Wasn't she woman enough to do what had to be done, to find out once and for all if she could? If he could? She surfaced, her eyes closed, wondering if he would come swimming after her again—and if he did, whether she would try to escape.

The sun was hot on her face. She moved her arms and her tail only slightly, holding herself where she floated. Was he watching her? Was he fantasizing about the mermaid, or was he picturing her as she really was, without the concealing suit, without the long pants she always wore. How could he possibly know what she looked like? How could he begin to imagine what she had imagined every night since she had met him?

She let her tail sink and her head come erect. He was gone, and she wondered if maybe he really had gone to turn on the pumps that would drain the water. She listened and watched. There was no sound of a motor, and the water level remained the same. Maybe he had simply . . . gone. Maybe, for both their sakes, it was easier that way. Of course it was. He wouldn't have to suffer through the embarrassment of trying and failing, and she wouldn't have to suffer through the agony of seeing revulsion on his face.

But, oh, God! How she wanted to be beautiful for him. More than anything else, she wanted that, and there was nothing she could do to make it so. She was what she was. She thought she had faced it. She thought she had dealt with it. And then Mark Forsythe had come into her life and everything had changed. She was right back at square one, right back in the hospital when she looked down and saw the way the covers lay over her on the bed.

It had taken her days to find the courage, the strength, to sit up and push those covers down and look at herself. And it had taken her hours to

stop feeling nauseated each time she looked after
that.

Oh, over time she had learned to use her prosthesis, to walk with little more than a slight limp,
to wear clothing that hid from the world the fact
that she was no longer a complete person. She
actually had gone through a period of grieving for
her lost leg much the same as she had gone
through a period of grieving for her lost husband.
Her geologist sister and brother-in-law had come
home from Oklahoma to visit, and they had been
the first to see her with the prosthesis on, other
than the hospital staff and her mother. And she
remembered the look in her brother-in-law's eyes.

She knew he'd been wondering how he'd feel if
it were Kathy who had lost a leg; would he still be
able to go to bed with her? For the first time she
saw some good in her having lost Lance, because
how would she have felt if he had looked at her as
her brother-in-law had, with awful, horrified speculation in his eyes?

Her brother, four years her junior but wise in
ways that always had amazed her, had been the
first one to put it into proper perspective for her.
He'd said a lot of things, but the one thing she
remembered most was that if she'd known that
the choice was between her left leg from the knee
down, and the life of the fifteen-year-old boy she'd
flung herself across just in time, would she rather
have lost the student?

Of course put like that, loss of her leg paled into insignificance.

Many of her fellow teachers had come to visit her, and nearly all of her students. As she limped down the hospital corridor, practicing, learning to walk all over again, she had seen the looks of pity. And when she had gone back to school, it had been even worse. She couldn't teach physical education when it was all she could do to stay upright, and she accepted that. There were other things she was qualified to teach, but it was the counseling she couldn't handle. How could she adequately counsel hurt or frightened or maladjusted children, when she herself was so miserably maladjusted and living in constant terror?

But what hurt the most was when she had overheard herself referred to as the teacher with the wooden leg.

Mermaiding was a watery haven, where no one ever guessed that she had about as much grace on land as did a sea lion.

She saw Mark returning, wearing his shorts again, and discovered she still wasn't ready to talk to him. She ducked under once more, but she was tiring and she knew it. She couldn't hold her breath and stay down as long as she'd been able to ten minutes ago, and it was getting harder and harder to make her thighs swing that tail around.

She popped up to gasp in a breath and heard something land close beside her. Opening her eyes, she blinked until she could see, and discovered a small bottle with a paper rolled up inside it floating near her. She clutched it in her hand, staring at it, afraid to open it, afraid to look up, but when she did look up, Mark was gone again. All that remained was the note.

Intrigued, she opened it and carefully took it out with her wet fingers.

No more games, Mermaid. When you're
ready, holler. I'll be listening.
I love you.

Jillian swam back to the edge of the pool and then went to the steps at the shallow end. Hitching herself up, she sat there for a long time, thinking, feeling the water running out of her hair and down her back, feeling love and fear and hope and desire all warring within her. She lay back on the hot slates of the pool deck and stared at the green branches of a tree against the deep blue of the sky, remembering the look on Mark's face when she had told him.

Had it been shocked horror over the fact that she was incomplete, less than a whole woman, or had it been shocked horror that the woman he loved had been injured so grievously?

There was also one other possibility that she had to face. Could he have been horrified because she thought so little of him, put so little faith in the strength of his love? If she had learned that he was disabled, would it make any difference to her? Would she love him less? Want him less?

No. And if he had thought that of her, she'd have been more than horrified. She'd have been hurt and angry and wouldn't have wasted nearly as much time pandering to him as he had pandering to her.

Slowly she sat up. She wanted to holler. That was what he'd said to do, but her throat was tight with fear, and all she could manage was a soft plea. "Mark?"

He materialized. Crouching at her side, he didn't touch her. He just said, "I'm here, Jillian."

"Will you please help me out of this suit?"

"Sure," he said huskily. "Just tell me what to do."

"At the back there's a strip held down with Velcro. Under that is a zipper."

He put his arms around her, lifted her as he stood, and started to walk. Her startled gaze flew to his face. "Where are we going?"

"Inside. When I get you out of this suit, Mermaid, I am going to make mad, passionate, and very thorough love to you until you are so fully convinced that no matter what kind of accident might have befallen you, I love you and want you and find you the most captivating, beautiful woman on earth. And because that's what you are to me, the moment I get you naked, I'm not going to be able to wait, and I thought we might be more comfortable in my bed."

She put her hand around his face and turned it so he had to meet her gaze. "Where the shades can be drawn and the lights turned off and the covers pulled right up high?"

He looked at her and shook his head. "For your sake, if that's what you need, I'm willing to have it that way, but I hadn't thought of that, Jillian."

"Hadn't you, Mark? Aren't you even a little bit afraid that you might not like what you see?"

He smiled confidently. "Nope. Not for one minute."

Tears flooded her eyes. "Well, dammit, it worries me, let me tell you."

"I know. And I wish it didn't. And I also think that in the not very distant future, it's not going to worry you any longer." He bent his head and touched his lips to hers. "And now, can we go to bed?"

"Mark . . . no drawn shades. No turned-out lamps. No concealing sheets and blankets. N-not for my sake." She swallowed hard and drew in a deep, unsteady breath, and he watched her chin jut out as if anticipating a blow. "For my sake, do it here," she said, aware that her teeth were chattering. "T-take me out of my suit right here. In, as they say, the . . . the light of the noonday sun."

"Do they say that?" he asked conversationally as he sat her down again on the side of the pool and fumbled at the back of her suit.

"I don't really know." Her voice shook. "But I thought it sounded impressive."

"Oh, it did." The zipper slid down, revealing the

back of a skin tight black bathing suit. "Very impressive." He peeled the neoprene suit down to her waist, and she lifted up so he could slide it off her thighs and down over the rest of her.

Then, as if she had run out of courage, she followed the suit down into the pool, the ripples on the surface masking her deformity. She sat there in her black bathing suit, looking straight ahead, her face pale, her eyes dark with fear and pain.

Mark stripped out of his shorts again and dropped down to the lower step with her, taking her taut face in his hands, feeling her clenched jaws, and seeing the stark terror in her eyes.

"Do you know that I love you?" he whispered.

She nodded, unable to speak.

"Do you know that I want you the way I've never wanted anyone before?"

She only looked at him, feeling doubt and hope and love all tangled up inside her again. With infinite care, he bent and brushed his lips over hers, just touching them. Then once more he kissed her, with only a hint more force. The tip of his tongue brushed over her lower lip, and a shiver went right through her as her nipples tightened, sending urgent messages to the very heart of her.

She drew in a shaky breath and lifted her hands to his chest, letting her fingers rest on the thick pelt of hair that lay wet and glistening with beads of moisture. "That . . . that must be pretty close to the way I want you," she said shakily as rain-bows danced before her eyes.

She met his mouth with her own, her arms sliding around his torso to pull him close, closer, until her breasts were against the hardness of his chest. It was grand. It was wonderful. It was the way it was supposed to be.

He rocked her against his body, rubbing his skin over hers, and then slid one hand down under her bottom, lifting her until she floated onto his thighs.

"Mark . . ." she said with a sob moments later, gasping for breath as she rested her forehead against his chest. "How can you do that to me with just a kiss?"

He took her hand and moved it down until it curled around the hardness of him. "How can you do that to me simply by smiling?" he asked, and then groaned as her fingers tightened, and she stroked the long, heated hardness of him until he snatched himself out of her grasp. "Stop, love, it's too fast."

While she contented herself with discovering the hard little nipples that hid within the swirls of hair on his chest, he slipped her bathing suit down to bare her breasts, dipping his head to take first one then the other nipple deeply into his mouth. His hands encircled her slim waist. leaning her back in the water so that her hair floated in a soft cloud all around her shoulders. Standing on the lower level of the shallow end, he pulled her up until her thighs were around him, and bent to her breast again.

"Mark." Her soft moan was made half in pleasure, half in protest. "What if . . . will anybody come?"

He laughed and murmured in her ear, making her laugh at the very obvious reply he gave her, and suddenly everything was right.

"But not right away," he added. "Not for a long time, my darling. We are going to make this last and last until I have given you every drop of pleasure you can stand."

As he returned to her mouth, covering it with his own and plunging inside with his tongue, he caught two fistfuls of cloth and dragged her suit right off her. When she felt the cool water and his hands caressing her buttocks, she thought she would faint from delight. His fingers knew exactly what to do, and in moments she was sure she'd endured the last drop of pleasure she could stand—but he showed her again and again that there was more and that she could take it, that she wanted it.

Just as his hands knew what to do, his mouth knew where next to kiss her. Eyes, ears, throat, shoulders, the hollow of her elbow, the undersides of her breasts all received attention. And then as he sat her on the second step once more and dipped his head underwater, he kissed her navel and the tops of her thighs, parting them so that his darting tongue could send her into a frenzy of passion.

She pulled him up before he drowned and gave him mouth to mouth resuscitation.

"You are so beautiful," he said moments later when he could breathe again. Lifting her astride his lap, he held her breasts to his cheeks, rubbing them gently with his slight stubble until she was crying out for him to stop.

"Mark, love me, please," she said, shaking so hard that she couldn't even cling to him anymore, so hard that he had to hold her to him to keep her from drifting away. "I need you. Please, Mark, love me now."

With both hands, she captured him and drew him to her. He lifted her and drove inside her in one thrust, and then they were one, staring into each other's eyes as the slow, stately dance began.

Ten

It was like flying through water, slow and sweet and graceful, as they moved together, creating a rushing sensation like nothing she had ever experienced, a deep, inner storm that flooded through her in ever-increasing waves, shaking her, rocking her, making her cry out with the intensity of it. Closing her eyes, she flung her head back. He drew one of her nipples into his mouth while she drew him deeper within her body. He was all hard pulsing power, filling her, fulfilling her as her muscles tightened around him. It seemed it would never end as Mark rode the swirling currents with her, soaring high, plunging low, then rising again until they shuddered together in joint spasms of ecstasy that carried them over the top and let them coast slowly down to a quiet shore.

"Sweetheart?" Languidly Jillian rolled her head on his wet chest.

"Hmm?"

"Are you all right?"

She snuggled her face into the hollow between his shoulder and his neck, tasting him, smelling him, loving him. "I don't think so. I don't think I'll ever be the same again."

"I know I won't."

"So much for courage," she said, still hiding from him. "So much for the light of the noonday sun."

"I think that was originally about mad dogs and Englishmen going out in it, but not necessarily naked."

"Um-hmm. I guess so." Still she felt ashamed of her cowardice. She loved this man. Why was it so hard to show him all of herself, all of her naked, imperfect self?

"Jillian, I understand, you know. This must have been very difficult for you. It was the first time, wasn't it? Since—"

Silently she nodded.

He smoothed her wet hair back from her face, kissed the top of her head. "Do you know how honored I feel that you've given me so much love, so much trust?"

She felt a sob rising up in her chest and choked it down. Now was not the time for tears. That time was past. It was a time for rejoicing, and she lifted her face to his, her eyes aglow.

"I love you, Mark. Did I tell you how much I love you?" Then, shy again, remembering that she had said those words over and over just moments before, she dipped her head once more and hugged him tightly.

He chuckled. The sound was deep in his chest and rumbled pleasantly against her ear and filled her heart with gladness. "It seems to me that I did hear you mention it a time or two. But you're free to say it as often as you like."

"You won't get bored with hearing it?"

"I won't get bored with anything you do." He lifted her face and looked at her. "You've made me so happy, Jilly. Is it okay for me to call you Jilly? I mean, your mother does, but . . ."

"All my family does, Mark." She touched his face and brushed her fingers over his lips. "I mean, all the *rest* of my family."

When she awoke in Mark's bed, she knew many hours had passed. Through the open drapes, she could see that twilight had faded the sky to white, and inked in the trees as black silhouettes. She was tangled in the sheet he'd pulled over them after they'd made love again. One light burned at the bedside, and in its pale glow, she could see that he wasn't in the room. She sat up, put on her prosthesis that was next to the bed, and called, "Mark?"

There was no reply, so she got out of bed and with

the aid of a chair, went into the adjoining bathroom where they had showered together earlier. He had left her a note saying that he'd be back soon. No word of where he'd gone, just that he'd be back. Oddly enough it was all she needed to know.

Smiling, she saw that he had left out another white terry robe for her. How many did he own? She still had that first one at her house. She took a quick bath and wrapped herself in the warm, thick garment, which came only to her knees. Her eyes widened and her heart started to hammer when a door slammed somewhere in the house, and she heard Mark's footsteps approaching.

"Jillian?" He had seen the empty bed. "Jillian, where are you?"

She opened the bathroom door and stood there, holding onto the knob, watching him cross toward her, a suitcase in one hand, and a world of love in his eyes. Slowly she breathed again, not realizing until then that she had been holding her breath, waiting for some kind of reaction from him—one that never came.

His gaze swept over her from the top of her head to the tips of her toes, and still all she could see in his face was the warmth of love that made her complete even in her own eyes and suffused her with gladness.

"Hi," he said, and kissed her until she was dizzy.

"Where have you been?"

He grinned. "Mmm. I like that. You sound like a

wife already. It's going to be wonderful having someone care about where I go and what I do and when I come home. And, since I have permission to marry you, you have my permission to sound like a wife."

She had to laugh. "Of all the evasive, sneaky answers I've ever heard, that beats them all. You still didn't tell me where you—What do you mean, you have permission to marry me? Whose?"

"Your mother's and your daughter's. Your mother packed some things she thought you'd need tonight. I've already checked. She packed a couple of things you won't need, too, but she meant well."

He lifted her with one arm and carried her to the bed where he handed her the bag. "You get dressed. I'm going to fire up the barbecue."

She grinned. "Now you're starting to sound just like a husband. Bossy. Domineering."

Leaning casually in the doorway, he looked her up and down as if imagining her without the thick bathrobe covering her. His gaze made her tingle. "Just getting in practice," he said with a grin, then asked, "When?"

Drawing in a tremulous breath, she said, "Yesterday?"

He laughed. "I'll work on it, Mermaid. I want it to be that soon too."

"Talk about a whirlwind romance!" Jillian, who sat on the arm of a chair in the living room of their Seattle home, set the phone down with one hand while the other stroked through Mark's thick hair. "Do you know who that was?"

He smiled. "Well, the impression I got is that it was your mother, and that she's getting married. I can't say I'm surprised. That day I went there to get your things for the night, I discovered that Edward had canceled his dinner date with his daughter because he'd finally met his match in Scrabble and didn't want to leave. I take it they're well-matched in other ways, as well."

"But Mark! They've known each other for a month and a half! Six weeks! And they're getting married!"

He tumbled her onto his lap and nuzzled his face into her neck, sending shivers of delight down her spine. "And who are you to talk, Mrs. Forsythe? What about us? We were married four weeks after we met."

She laughed as she responded soberly, "That was different. We were never strangers."

"Maybe Shirley and Edward feel the same way," he said. But as she responded to the growing urgency of his kisses and touches, adding a few embellishments of her own as they went along, he didn't think so. Nobody but he and Jillian had ever felt quite this way about each other. Nobody could have, or the world already would have come to a halt.

In the few weeks that they'd been married, it seemed that all they ever did, ever wanted to do—

and ever would want to do—every chance they got was love each other.

He carried her off to their bedroom, closing the door tightly and setting her down gently in the middle of their big bed. She sighed in perfect happiness as they began to take each other's clothes off, and then murmured in ecstasy as their bodies finally came together in a wonderful union they had made uniquely theirs.

While the nights belonged to them, their days belonged to their children. Sleeping in was a luxury they had been denied after their brief, week-long honeymoon. But as Mark got up to open the door to a knock the next morning, and Jillian sat against the headboard smiling at the two kids who stood in the doorway, neither of them minded.

"This is the last day of your vacation, Dad. What are we going to do?"

Chris, under the umbrella of love spread by his father and stepmother and little stepsister, had become a changed child. He still grieved for his mother but no longer believed that Mark deliberately had killed her or had wanted him out of the way too. As he'd said to Jillian one day when the two of them were talking quietly together about it, "I think I was a little bit nuts, Jilly. I just missed my mom so much, and I was scared to love Dad in case he went away too."

"It's the last day of yours and Amber's vacations too," said Mark, the sound of his voice bringing Jillian back to the present. "Suppose the two of you decide and then let us know."

As the kids left, he closed the door and clicked the lock in place. Turning back to the bed, he shucked his pajama bottoms and slid back under the covers, drawing his wife into his embrace. The decision-making, he was certain, would take at least half an hour.

That would be long enough—just.

Jillian looked at the clean bathroom and backed out of it. It was the last room of the eight she had scrubbed or vacuumed to within an inch of its life, and there was nothing more to do. It was only eleven-fifteen in the morning. The day stretched ahead of her endlessly, as had all the other days except weekends, for the past three months. The Thanksgiving festivities were behind them, and her Christmas shopping was all done. The packages were all wrapped and stored neatly away. She had read all the books she'd been wanting to read for years, watched a hundred or more movies on the VCR. Next, she supposed, were daytime game shows and soaps. Wandering into the spotless kitchen, she spent an hour baking cookies then another twenty minutes cleaning up again.

She sighed, sat down, and idly turned the pages of a magazine. She could go shopping, she thought, but she didn't need anything. She didn't want anything. Neither of the kids needed anything. Mark didn't need anything. Nobody did.

But more important, nobody needed her for anything at all.

She sat blinking hard to hold back tears as she let that thought sink in, but the tears flowed anyway.

That was the whole problem, wasn't it? She was redundant in all their lives.

The kids had school all day. Chris went to soccer practice a couple of afternoons a week, guitar lessons once a week, and the other days he was out playing with his friends.

And Amber went to school, to ballet and karate, and talked about her teachers and how wonderful they were. She had made lots of friends in the months they had been there and was one busy little girl.

Mark, of course, had his work. While his "elves" were excellent at the jobs they did, they still needed supervision and guidance, so Mark didn't take very many days off, even though he could afford to. He had an able assistant who could and did take over when necessary, but his workers trusted him, looked up to him, and he liked to be there for them.

She and Mark had a fairly normal social life, and from within his circle of friends, she had made some friends of her own.

But going out to lunch with a friend once or twice a week wasn't what she wanted. It wasn't what she needed. Now, in this moment of tearful introspection, she asked herself what it was she needed, but she couldn't come up with an easy answer, only one that she recognized as being impossible.

She needed a job, but she hadn't seen any ads for mermaids in a long while.

She quickly brushed her tears away as she heard Mark's key in the door. But as he entered, he frowned, knowing right away that she had been crying. Crouching in front of her, he drew her into his arms. "What is it, love?"

She shook her head. If she didn't have an answer for herself, how could she give one to her husband?

"Nothing, really. Just a minor case of the blues. It'll get better," she assured him.

It didn't get any better. Day by day it got worse. Even the kids noticed and started tiptoeing around as if they had done something bad to make Jillian so sad. But she struggled to put on a cheerful demeanor for their sakes and Mark's. Often, she could convince the children that there was nothing bothering her, but Mark was a different story.

At night he held her, loved her, traveled with her to their secret, wonderful place, and then lay awake when she thought he was asleep, watching silent tears run down her face. But he couldn't get an answer out of her about what the problem was. Maybe it was just the adjustment to a different kind of life, to marriage, to being a homemaker, to having two children rather than one. Maybe she missed her mother.

And maybe he had been right all along, that he made a better bachelor than he did a husband, because clearly he wasn't making her happy. What they had together wasn't enough.

•   •   •

When Christmas came and her mother and Edward, the two children, and even Chris's grandparents sat down to dinner with them and complimented her on the wonderful job she had done, Mark thought perhaps it would be the turning point.

She glowed under their praise and watched with pride as Mark carved the golden-skinned turkey she had spent all afternoon basting and fretting over. On New Year's Eve, she laughed like an excited girl as she kissed him in the crowd of swaying, dancing friends, with streamers and confetti and music swirling around them, and he thought that now, at last, she had made the necessary adjustments and would be happy again.

But when the kids were back in school and Mark back at work, the sadness descended upon her once more, even though she was growing better at concealing it.

And then one evening when the children were in bed, and Mark and Jillian sat watching television together, it happened.

There it was. The boat, the bay, the white-clad fisherman playing his catch as his deep, persuasive voice said, "Our oceans are our most precious resource. Some of the smallest of earth's living creatures make their home here"—the screen filled with a much-magnified picture of phytoplankton—"as do the largest." Whales moved in stately splendor and the song of the blue whale came from the speakers.

The voice went on, overriding the whale song, outlining the many ways in which the oceans were important to all mankind, while on the screen porpoises dove and played, schools of tropical fish darted here and there, boats bobbed on clean water, and children splashed and played on calm shores.

"And we do not know all there is to know about what lives in those mysterious depths," the resonant voice continued as the screen filled once more with the stern of the boat and the fisherman in white. All at once, a disturbance on the surface of the seething ocean was the focus of interest, and then a large, silver tail shot with blue and silver, followed by a sleek, golden head emerging from the water appeared, and Jillian Lockstead, Mermaid, was being seen by millions of viewers.

"How can we go on pouring tons of chemicals into these waters? How can we go on risking their purity—their already compromised purity—risking not only the lives of the creatures we know about, but those of whose existence we can only guess?"

As the smiling mermaid came nearer, reaching up to unhook the line from her costume, the camera drifted over her. She waved, flipped her tail, and then dove away out of sight.

"There is no such thing as a mermaid, many of you are saying," the candidate went on as the camera panned back to his earnest face. "But I say, do we know that for certain? And if such a beautiful, exotic creature should exist, can we risk killing her and her kind with our own careless acts of vandalism?"

He went on, but Mark heard nothing. He was watching Jillian's white face, seeing the tension there, the tears running down her cheeks as her shoulders heaved from the force of the sobs she was trying to hold back.

And now he understood.

He didn't touch her. He didn't hold her. He couldn't comfort her. He could only look on in torture as he witnessed her pain.

Finally he said, his voice just barely above a murmur, "It's not enough, is it? We aren't enough for you. Being my wife, the mother of our children, isn't enough. You want . . . *that* . . . back." He waved at the television screen where the camera was now following the mermaid's course as she swam back out to sea, turning now and then to wave and smile as if beckoning the world to follow.

They both watched as the scene switched to an underwater shot of the mermaid poised at the entrance to a grotto. She disappeared inside, leaving only an afterimage of magic that slowly faded as the candidate's voice faded, and a loud commercial came on extolling the virtues of a bathroom tile cleaner.

"You want the adulation. You want the panting, red faces pressed against the glass, the notes in your dressing room, the thrill of knowing that you're turning on five hundred men a night, the ego boost of knowing that every woman in your audience is envious of you," Mark accused.

"God, Jillian! How can I compete with that? What do I have to do to be enough for you? I took that all away from you, didn't I? And I haven't given you anything to make up for it."

He got to his feet and walked slowly to their bedroom, for the first time not reaching out his hand to draw her along with him. And for the first time he was asleep, or seemed to be, when she finally went to bed.

When morning came, Jillian stayed in bed, listening to the children squabbling, to Mark's shower beating against the wall near their bed, and then slowly got herself ready to face the day. At last alone in the house, she sat at the table in the kitchen, for the first time not leaping up to begin scouring and scrubbing and keeping the house spotless. She stared at the toast crumbs, at the milk splotches on the crisp tablecloth she had so carefully starched and ironed even though the instructions said ironing was not required. She stared at the dirty dishes and thought long and hard about what Mark had said the previous night.

He was right. It wasn't enough. She had thought that having him as a husband, having their two children to raise, their home to care for, would be enough. She had believed, so wrongly, that all it would take to make her complete was Mark and his love. And now she knew she had been wrong.

She was still as incomplete as she had been—as she had become—the day that double-barreled, sawed-off shotgun had torn half her leg from her body.

She was still as incomplete as she had been while dressed in the suit that gave her the appearance of completeness, that created an illusion of reality, but was, when it came right down to it, only a fantasy, something to hide behind.

For more than two years she had let herself buy that fantasy because it was easier than facing up to a cruel truth. It was her mind that was incomplete, not her body.

She showered, dressed very carefully, and with trepidation but determination, got into the car Mark had given her as a wedding gift—one with no rust, one on which no rust would ever dare to appear—and pulled out of the garage. At the street she hesitated for another moment, wondering if she could go through with her plan. Then she turned the car and headed downtown.

"Mrs. Lockstead! What are you doin' here?"

Jillian turned in response to the surprised voice. She smiled and blinked in astonishment. "Hello, Juan." She had to look up at him now. In two and a half years he had grown so much. "Still hangin' in, are you? A senior this year?"

He shook his head. "Nope. Junior again. I screwed up pretty bad and had to do last year's stuff over again, but this time round, it's easier."

"Good for you for sticking with it. I'm happy for you. I always knew you could do it."

She moved on, haltingly, because so many of the students in the crowded hallways remembered her and stopped to talk, to tell her what they'd done while she'd been away, and to ask about her life. A few had even seen the paid political announcement in which she had appeared and asked if she was going to be on TV all the time.

For several minutes she stood outside the gym, hearing the sounds of a basketball game going on behind the closed doors, the shrill, feminine voices, the slap, slap, slap of a dribbled ball, the thud of feet landing on hardwood. She ached to open the door and watch, but as the halls emptied and classes resumed, she walked on.

Finally she made it to the office. One of the secretaries burst into tears upon seeing her and gave her a hug. The other two were new and didn't know her, didn't remember except vaguely. She was a figure from an old, mostly forgotten newspaper story, a thirty-second segment on the evening news. There had been so many other news items, the one concerning her had been buried in the memories of those not intimately involved.

When she was ushered into the principal's office, he got slowly to his feet.

"Well, Jillian." He didn't smile.

"Hello, Peter. You told me—two years ago—if I was ever ready to come back to let you know. That you'd put in a good word for me with the board. Will you do that now?"

"By my reckoning, it's been closer to three years. Two and a half and then some."

"Okay, so call me a liar for seven months. It took me a while to make up my mind."

"Are you sure you're ready?"

She gazed at him steadily. "I'm sure."

He continued to look at her, from the top of her neatly combed hair, to her dark blue dress with its stand-up white collar, to her legs which were clad in navy stockings. The hem of the dress hung to mid-calf, but even that and the dark hose didn't completely disguise the fact that she wore a prosthesis.

"Yes," he said. And now he smiled. "You're ready."

"Are there—do you know if there are any openings?"

"In this school?" She could sense his doubt of the wisdom in that.

"In this school," she said firmly.

He didn't reply, only took her arm and walked her across the office to a door which she recalled led to a small interview room. Opening it, he let her enter then stood behind her, gazing over her shoulder at the sullen, pimply-faced girl who sat slumped in a chair.

"This is Star. Star, this is Mrs. Lockstead."

"Mrs. Forsythe now," Jillian said, moving toward the other chair and sinking into its softness. "What's up, Star?"

"Why ask?" The girl didn't even look at Jillian. "You don't give a damn."

Jillian leaned forward, her elbows on her knees,

her chin on her hands, and looked the girl square in the eyes. "If I didn't give a damn," she said pleasantly, "I wouldn't be in this room."

Behind her, she heard Peter close the door quietly.

Just as quietly Jillian got down to business— her business, the business of trying to get through to a child who didn't want to be gotten through to.

She felt good all of a sudden, equal to the challenge. She felt useful. She felt whole.

"Jillian! Where have you been?" Mark's face was gray, his eyes haunted. "I came home early because we have to talk, and you weren't here. No one knew where you were. None of your friends, none of the neighbors. "I was . . . afraid," he went on. "Afraid you'd left me."

"No!" She went to him, slid her arms around his waist, and slowly his came around her. She smiled up at him. "Never. I'd never leave you. I had something important to do, Mark, and I didn't expect you to be waiting. I'm sorry, darling. I didn't mean to worry you."

"You did more than worry me. You terrified me. I guess I've gotten used to your always being here. You've become so important to me that I panic if I don't know where you are. And lately you've been . . . unhappy. It made me unhappy, too, Jilly, because I thought I was the one making you that way. Last night when I realized that you missed your job, I overreacted. I'm sorry, sweetheart. You have every right to do what ever you want to do. If you want to get another job, that's fine. I'll handle it. If it means sharing you with five hundred ogling men, so be it. As long as it's me you come home to each night."

She looked up at him and stroked his face, trying to erase the frown between his eyes, the lines of tension around his mouth. He caught her hand and kissed her palm. "I'll always come home to you, Mark, and yes, I do want to get another job. In fact, I have one."

He looked into her glowing face, seeing the happiness that had been missing for so long, and something inside him ripped in half. He wanted the happiness to remain on her face, loved to see her mouth curved into a beguiling smile, rejoiced to see the pink color of her cheeks, the light in her eyes.

"You won't have to share me with five hundred ogling men," she told him, holding him tightly, her hands moving into his hair, luxuriating in its softness. "But if you think you can stand to share me with twenty-five hundred high school students, then you've got yourself a working wife."

"Jillian?" He lifted her into his arms and carried her to the couch where he sat down with her on his lap, her legs stretched out on the cushions beside him. He stroked down one leg then up the other, his calluses catching on navy blue nylon as his hand slid up under the hem of her dress. "Are you sure?"

She nestled into his embrace. "Is the sky blue? Is—" She kissed him for a long time and then leaned her head back comfortably on his shoulder. She glanced at her watch. There was still an hour and a half before Amber was due home from school.

He caught the look on her face and gently tipped her back until she lay on the couch, then covered her body with his own. It was a long time before they stood up and walked together, clothes bundled under their arms, into their bedroom to shower and change before the kids came home.

Standing in the pelting water, Mark smoothed her wet hair back from her face and watched as it clung to her neck and shoulders, wisping in wet curls over her high, proud breasts. Her mouth was curved in a smile, the little freckles on her nose had paled during the winter but her eyes shone, sea-green and glowing with happiness, lit with the sunshine that lived in her soul.

"Welcome back, my magic mermaid," he whispered as he bent to kiss her. "Welcome back."

THE EDITOR'S CORNER

Get Ready For
A SPECTACULAR LOVESWEPT SUMMER
★★★★★★★★★★★★★★★★★★★★★★★★★★★★★★★

Next month we kick off one of LOVESWEPT's most sizzling summers! First, we bring you just what you've been asking for—

•

LOVESWEPT GOLDEN CLASSICS

•

We are ushering in this exciting program with four of the titles you've most requested by four of your most beloved authors . . .

Iris Johansen's
THE TRUSTWORTHY REDHEAD
(Originally published as LOVESWEPT #35)

•

Billie Green's
TEMPORARY ANGEL
(Originally published as LOVESWEPT #38)

•

Fayrene Preston's
THAT OLD FEELING
(Originally published as LOVESWEPT #45)

•

Kay Hooper's
SOMETHING DIFFERENT
(Originally published as LOVESWEPT #46)

•

With stunning covers—richly colored, beautifully enhanced by the golden signatures of the authors—LOVESWEPT'S GOLDEN CLASSICS are pure pleasure for those of you who missed them five years ago and exquisite "keepers" for the libraries of those who read and loved them when they were first published. Make sure your bookseller holds a set just for you or order the CLASSICS through our LOVESWEPT mail order subscription service.

And now a peek at our six new sensational romances for next month.

We start off with the phenomenal Sandra Brown's **TEMPER-ATURES RISING**, LOVESWEPT #336. Handsome Scout Ritland is celebrating the opening of a hotel he helped build on a lush South Pacific island when he's lured into a garden by an extraordinarily beautiful woman. But Chantal duPont has more in *(continued)* mind than a romantic interlude on this sultry moonlit night. She wants Scout all right—but to build a bridge, a bridge to connect the island on which she grew up with the mainland. Then there's an accident that Chantal never intended and that keeps Scout her bedridden patient. In the shadow of an active volcano the two discover their fierce hunger for each other . . . and the smoldering passion between them soon explodes with far-reaching consequences. This is Sandra Brown at her best in a love story to cherish. And remember—this wonderful romance is also available in a Doubleday hardcover edition.

Since bursting onto the romance scene with her enormously popular **ALL'S FAIR** (remember the Kissing Bandit?), Linda Cajio has delighted readers with her clever and sensual stories. Here comes an especially enchanting one, **DESPERATE MEASURES**, LOVESWEPT #337. Ellen Kitteridge is an elegant beauty who draws Joe Carlini to her as iron draws a magnet. Wild, virile, Joe pursues her relentlessly. Ellen is terrified because of her early loveless marriage to a treacherous fortune hunter. She runs from Joe, hides from him . . . but she can't escape. And Joe is determined to convince her that her shattered past has nothing to do with their thrilling future together. Linda's **DESPERATE MEASURES** will leave you breathless!

That brilliant new star of romance writing Deborah Smith gives you another thrilling story in *The Cherokee Trilogy*, **TEMPTING THE WOLF**, LOVESWEPT #338. This is the unforgettable tale of a brilliant, maverick Cherokee who was a pro football player and is now a businessman. Of most concern to Erica Gallatin, however, is his total (and threatening) masculinity. James is dangerous, perfection molded in bronze, absolutely irresistible—and he doesn't trust beautiful "non-Indian" women one bit! Erica is determined to get in touch with her heritage as she explores the mystery of Dove's legacy . . . and she's even more determined to subdue her mad attraction to the fierce warrior who is stealing her soul. This is a romance as heartwarming as it is heart-stopping in its intensity.

Judy Gill produces some of the most sensitive love stories we publish. In LOVESWEPT #339, **A SCENT OF ROSES**, she will once again capture your emotions with the exquisite romance of a memorable hero and heroine. Greg Miller is a race car driver who's lost his memory in an accident. His wife, Susan, puts past hurts aside when she agrees to help him recover. At his family's home in the San Juan Islands—a setting made for love—they rediscover the passion they shared . . . but can they

(continued)

compromise on the future? A thrilling story of deep passion and deep commitment nearly destroyed by misunderstanding.

It's always our greatest pleasure to discover and present a brand-new talent. Please give a warm, warm welcome to Courtney Henke, debuting next month with **CHAMELEON,** LOVESWEPT #340. This is a humorous yet emotionally touching romance we suspect you will never forget . . . in large measure because of its remarkable hero. Emma Machlen is a woman with a single purpose when she invades Maxwell Morgan's domain. She's going to convince the cosmetics mogul to buy the unique fragrance her family has developed. She's utterly desperate to make the sale. But she never counts on the surprises Max will have for her, not the least of which is his incredible attractiveness. Enchanted by Emma, drawn to her against his will, Max is turned upside down by this little lady whom he *must* resist. Emma has her work cut out for her in winning over Max . . . but the poor man never has a chance! An absolutely wonderful story!

And what could make for more sizzling reading than another of Helen Mittermeyer's Men of Fire? Nothing I can think of. All the passion, intensity, emotional complexity, richness, and humor you expect in one of Helen's love stories is here in **WHITE HEAT,** LOVESWEPT #341. When Pacer Dillon—that irresistible heartbreaker Helen introduced you to before—meets Colm Fitzroy, he is dead set on taking over her family business. She's dead set on stopping him. Irresistible force meets immovable object. Colm is threatened now, having been betrayed in the past, and Pacer is just the man to save her while using the sweet, hot fire of his undying love to persuade her to surrender her heart to him. Pure dynamite!

Enjoy all our LOVESWEPTs—new and old—next month! And please remember that we love to hear from you.

Sincerely,

Carolyn Nichols

Carolyn Nichols
Editor
LOVESWEPT
Bantam Books
666 Fifth Avenue
New York, NY 10103

THE DELANEY DYNASTY

Men and women whose loves and passions are so glorious it takes many great romance novels by three bestselling authors to tell their tempestuous stories.

THE SHAMROCK TRINITY